"Just because I wasn't consulted before you were brought on board, don't think for a second that I haven't verified you can actually pull this off. This film is my responsibility, and Rebecca falls outside *your* known range."

Cait's jaw tightened. *Oh, he'd hit a nerve with that one.*

She recovered quickly, though. She always did. She stood and stepped away from the bench before turning on him. "You know, if you spent more time actually working, and less time playing beach blanket bingo in Europe, you might not have to find out what's happening with your own projects after the fact."

The disdain in her voice chased off any desire he'd had to play nice. Where did Cait get off, acting all high and mighty? "So you've been keeping up with my love-life? That's kind of… sad, actually."

"Oh, please. Would you get over yourself? The last thing I care about is who you're sleeping with now. I'm here for one reason and one reason only. And, believe me, it doesn't have a damn thing to do with you."

Dear Reader

Writing this letter to you makes me quite sad, as it means that my time with the Marshall family has come to an end. There's always a little twinge of that every time I say goodbye to characters—by this point in the process I've spent so much time with them that it's hard to let them go. But the Marshall brothers have been with me for three books now—almost a year of my life—and I'm feeling this loss a little harder than usual.

I adore all three Marshall brothers equally, but Finn holds a special place in my heart. He's the black sheep, the wild child, the one no one really understands but everyone can't help but love. While these traits are part of what makes Finn so irresistible, they also made it hard for me to figure out who his heroine would be. She couldn't be your average girl-next-door. Finn needed a heroine who wouldn't be overly impressed by his fame and fortune, or fazed by his fast-lane celebrity lifestyle. She had to be able to keep up, and connect with him personally and professionally. Cait met all my criteria nicely—*and* brought the sparks into this story!

I hope you enjoy Finn and Cait's adventure, and that the Marshall brothers have been as much fun for you to read about as they were for me to write.

All my best

Kimberly

REDEMPTION OF
A HOLLYWOOD
STARLET

BY
KIMBERLY LANG

First published in Great Britain 2012
by Mills & Boon, an imprint of Harlequin (UK) Limited.
Harlequin (UK) Limited, Eton House, 18-24 Paradise Road,
Richmond, Surrey TW9 1SR

© Kimberly Kerr 2012

ISBN: 978 0 263 22701 7

Harlequin (UK) policy is to use papers that are natural, renewable and recyclable products and made from wood grown in sustainable forests. The logging and manufacturing process conform to the legal environmental regulations of the country of origin.

Printed and bound in Great Britain
by CPI Antony Rowe, Chippenham, Wiltshire

Kimberly Lang hid romance novels behind her textbooks in junior high, and even a Master's programme in English couldn't break her obsession with dashing heroes and happily-ever-after. A ballet dancer turned English teacher, Kimberly married an electrical engineer and turned her life into an ongoing episode of *When Dilbert Met Frasier*. She and her Darling Geek live in beautiful North Alabama, with their one Amazing Child—who, unfortunately, shows an aptitude for sports.

Visit Kimberly at www.booksbykimberly.com for the latest news—and don't forget to say hi while you're there!

Recent titles by the same author:

THE POWER AND THE GLORY

Kimberly also writes for Mills & Boon® RIVA™. Her titles include:

THE PRIVILEGED AND THE DAMNED
GIRLS' GUIDE TO FLIRTING WITH DANGER

**Did you know these are also available as eBooks?
Visit www.millsandboon.co.uk**

Happy first birthday to James,
my gorgeous, brilliant and sweet nephew.

I have every confidence that
you will grow up to be a hero.

CHAPTER ONE

HE'D only been gone for three weeks. When he'd left, everything for this film had been fine and in place, but a mere twenty-one days later he'd returned to find the entire project sliding into hell.

Finn Marshall sat back in his chair in the trailer that served as their temporary offices while they were on location here in Maryland and rubbed a hand over his eyes. He was jetlagged and had hoped to have a couple of hours of sleep before he had to be in D.C. for the fundraiser tonight, but that wasn't looking to be in his cards. He had to sort out this God-awful mess first, and the more he heard, the less likely it seemed he'd even make it to his brother's in time to shower first.

Dolby Martin, his partner in Dolfinn Pictures, seemed remarkably upbeat for someone who had just rammed the *Titanic* into the iceberg. "We've been filming for a week now, and we're almost back on schedule."

Finn took a deep breath and tried to remember it would do no good at all to punch Dolby in the mouth. "And you saw no reason to tell me any of this while it was unfolding?"

"You needed to concentrate on getting us those permissions to shoot, and really there was nothing you could do from Monaco, anyway."

"I could have talked Cindy down."

"After Farrell told her he'd seen better acting in low-budget porn? Sorry, Finn, not even you could have charmed that snake back into the basket." Dolby shrugged. "Personally, though, I wasn't sad to see her go. I'll bet Cindy's in rehab before the premiere, and would you really want *that* hanging over the release?"

Dolby had a point, as much as Finn hated to admit it. Cindy had been perfect for the part of Rebecca: the right looks and a strong talent, coupled with a name guaranteed to get attention without overshadowing the leads. She'd sworn that she was clean the day they'd signed the contract, but he'd seen this story too many times before.

Maybe it was for the best. Technically, Dolby and the director had done the right thing, finding a replacement quickly and getting her on the next plane to Baltimore so that production was not shut down for long. On a professional level, Finn should be pleased. He should even be personally touched that Dolby understood the importance of this film to him and had reacted quickly to mitigate the damages. But Cait Reese? He shook his head. *Focus on what's important.*

"Caitlyn has been a real life-saver and a complete pro. She had her script memorized in days and jumped straight into rehearsals. Wait until you see what we have in the can already. She's perfect for Rebecca. Better than Cindy, even."

Finn didn't necessarily agree. The Cait he remembered was too primal and wild. She'd been able to channel that into light frothy characters, but the earthy, quiet strength of Rebecca? It had been three years, but…

"Trust me, Finn. You're going to be really pleased."

"If you honestly believed that, you wouldn't have signed her to *Folly* behind my back." He picked up his phone and scrolled through the voice mail messages. "Naomi is fit to be tied. You want to hear?"

"I've heard enough, thanks. Naomi doesn't want to share her spotlight with anyone. She's a real diva."

"That's a privilege she's earned and one we'll tolerate to keep her happy on this film."

Naomi Harte was one of the biggest names in Hollywood right now, and based on star power alone she had no reason to worry about anyone stealing any of her limelight. But this was personal for Naomi, too. She and Cait had launched at about the same time, and their rivalry went back to the years when they'd both still been playing teenagers in high-school romantic comedies and slasher films. Cait had always managed to stay a rung above Naomi on the ladder, though, her trajectory seemingly unstoppable until she'd flamed out so spectacularly. Many people said that Naomi wouldn't be where she was today if Cait hadn't left town when she had— and Naomi knew that. They were probably right.

"You know there's bad blood between Naomi and Cait. Did you intend to turn the set into a battlefield?"

Dolby snickered. "It's actually working out well. Naomi's real-life problems with Caitlyn make their on-screen animosity even more realistic."

"And Cait?" She wasn't one to keep her mouth closed or her opinions to herself.

"Is being far more adult about this. Caitlyn has been very up front about her desire to re-create herself and relaunch her career. *Folly* is the perfect vehicle for her return, and she's not too proud to admit that."

Folly might be perfect for Cait, but Cait might not be perfect for *Folly*. He wasn't in the business of providing starlets with second chances. Especially with a project like *Folly*. He had too much invested—professionally and personally—to let this become some kind of experiment.

"I'm still not sure Cait is the smart choice here."

"I gave Farrell full directorly discretion to find the right person for the role *and* make sure it was someone he could tolerate. Caitlyn was his choice, and unless she decides she wants out of her contract we're bound." Dolby shook his head in censure. "*I'm* not courting her parents' wrath because you don't want your ex on the set. I like my career, thanks very much."

Talk about having the tables turned. All his life he'd been the one no one wanted to cross out of fear of retaliation from his family. That was simply one of the perks of being a Marshall. But the Marshalls ruled the East Coast. In L.A., John Reese and Margaret Fields-Reese were the sitting monarchy. It wasn't false pride or ego to say that *he* was pretty damn influential in the business, but even he couldn't touch the power of Cait's parents. One day, maybe, but not today.

"Anyway," Dolby continued, "all reports indicate that Caitlyn is sober and stable now."

Caitlyn had never had a problem—beyond partying a little too hard—and he wasn't one to throw stones there. The press had just played it up until she'd looked like a good candidate for rehab in order to sell papers. She'd been all but set up to crash if she slipped even the tiniest bit. "I'm sure she is, but that won't stop the press from going insane with this."

Dolby's grin didn't help Finn's mood much. "The buzz is amazing. Between the return of the exiled princess and the possibility of a Naomi-Caitlyn catfight, everyone is talking about *Folly* already."

"That's not what I meant and you know it."

Dolby laughed. "You have to admit the possibility of a Finn and Caitlyn reunion will make all kinds of headlines."

"Which is exactly why you should have consulted me before you signed her."

"If we have to avoid your exes every time we try to cast a film, pretty soon there won't be an actress under thirty available to us."

But Cait wasn't just any ex. She was the one ex that made all his other exes look like good choices. The bitterness surprised him. "I don't want my personal life making more news than this project."

That sobered Dolby. "*Folly* will stand on its own."

Dolby was an idiot occasionally, but he, too, took pride in Dolfinn's reputation. *The Folly of the Fury* might be Finn's pet project, but Dolby was committed one hundred percent.

"I know it will, but since we just stepped into soap-opera-waiting-to-happen territory, I want everyone crystal-clear in their understanding of what will and won't fly around here. All the drama needs to be kept on camera."

"Agreed."

Finn sincerely hoped it would be that simple.

Caitlyn Reese breathed the humid night air deep into her lungs as the door swung shut behind her and the noise and lights of the party inside died as if she'd hit a mute button. She'd done well in there—she knew that—but she needed a few moments of relief from the stress of the evening. Looking around, she was happy to see that the terrace was deserted—not that she was surprised. Between the heat and the fact that anybody who was anyone was inside… The air-conditioning inside was almost worth the noise, but she crossed to the balustrade, anyway, and leaned against it as she exhaled.

She chuckled to herself when she realized her hands weren't quite steady. She'd been mingling at cocktail parties since before she could walk, so there was no real reason to let a simple fundraiser—regardless of the prestige of the guest list—to give her stage fright. And the crowd was friendly enough. Whatever they might think of her personally, no one was stupid enough to do anything that might limit their access to her parents and her parents' friends. There was way too much Hollywood money they'd like to see in their campaign coffers at stake for anyone to treat her with anything other than friendly respect.

Maybe a D.C. charity fundraiser peopled by the city's social register was exactly the right place for her to make her first official reappearance. Her plan was working out better than hoped for. She wanted to call someone and share her success, but she wasn't exactly close with anyone on this continent anymore, and it was the middle of the night in London. Her parents both happened to have releases this month, so they were on their respective junkets and she had no idea what their schedules were like. Even if she did have someone to call, she wasn't sure what she'd say. *My career may not be dead anymore?* Oh, well. She shrugged and smiled. *She* was still proud of herself.

"Miss Reese?"

Caitlyn turned to see that she wasn't alone now. The tall blond man she'd been speaking to earlier was approaching her with a cautious smile on his face. She racked her brain for his name. He worked for one of the congressmen, and he was a big fan of her parents' work, knew all of her movies… Bits of their conversation came back to her, but not his name. He'd been a little over-enthusiastic, bordering on creepy, and the fact they were now quite alone didn't sit well.

Be nice, but not too nice. "Hi, again."

"I saw you leaving." His forehead crinkled in concern. "Are you all right?"

"I'm fine. I just needed a little air. It's a little crowded in there."

He nodded. "It's a good turnout, so that's good for the fundraising part. But it does make it hard to really talk to people." The man stepped a little closer than was comfortable. Caitlyn eased back a step herself. "And I very much enjoyed talking to you."

She nodded slightly, not wanting to encourage him with anything more.

"In fact, I'd like to take you to dinner so we can get to know each other better."

Caitlyn kept her face neutral even as alarm bells began to clang faintly. *Don't overreact. Give him the benefit of the doubt.* She took another step back, anyway. "My schedule is quite tight, I'm afraid."

"How about tonight, then, since you're already here. There's a nice bistro not far away…"

She shook her head. *This shouldn't be happening here.* The guest list was very exclusive and supposedly kept situations like this from even coming up. "I'm sorry, but I can't."

He was not to be deterred by the gentle brush-off, though. Maybe she was overreacting, but the alarm bells rang louder as he leaned closer and she smelled the alcohol on his breath.

"Then we'll talk here."

"Actually, I was just about to go back inside when you caught me." She picked up her purse and indicated they should walk. "Shall we?"

"Miss Reese…" He didn't take the hint, so she moved past him. "Caitlyn, wait, damn it."

She was two steps past him when he caught her arm and tried to stop her with a too-tight-to-be-casual grip. At that moment he crossed the line. Her training kicked in, and a second later he was on his knees whimpering in pain from the way Caitlyn had his fingers pulled back. "Do *not* touch me. We don't know each other well enough for that, so it's quite rude."

"I just wanted to talk to you."

She tightened her grip just enough to make him gasp and understand that she was serious. "That's not going to happen. You're going to go back inside so that I don't have to have you arrested for assault and make a scene in front of all those people."

At his nod of assent she released his fingers and he flexed

his fingers experimentally. "No need to be such a bitch about it."

This was not what she'd signed on for tonight. "Go away. I'm done talking to you." She stepped away and pinned him with a stare that hopefully would convince him she meant business. The adrenaline pumping through her system left her shaky but energized.

"Caitlyn…"

"I think Cait was very clear in her instructions. I suggest you do as you were told."

The voice hit her like a brick wall. Her stomach sank at the same time electricity sizzled up her spine. *Damn, damn, damn.* This was *not* how she'd planned on seeing him again.

Maybe it wasn't him. It had been three years; she'd probably just confused his voice with a stranger's. She'd been tense about seeing him, and her mind was surely just playing tricks on her. *Because anything else would just be really unfair.* Holding on to that hope, Caitlyn looked over her shoulder as the owner of the voice emerged from the shadows.

Finn.

Great. What had she done to karma to deserve this? She just seemed destined to have Finn a part of all the times of her life she'd just like to forget.

At least Finn wouldn't blab about what he'd just witnessed to the papers. It was a small consolation, and Caitlyn grabbed on to it like a life raft in the swirl of emotions and memories that low, rich voice stirred up.

She could tell the guy—she still couldn't remember his name—recognized Finn, which wasn't surprising since Finn garnered almost as much press as the stars in the films he produced. And, of course, everyone on the planet knew about her past with Finn. The double whammy for her admirer, though, had to come from Finn's family ties: smart people didn't make enemies of the Marshalls. *Especially* if they wanted any kind of future in politics. They were simply too powerful a family to mess with.

But this guy, proving again he wasn't the sharpest knife in the drawer, got belligerent instead. "This is a private conversation, if you don't mind."

"Oh, I mind." Disdain dripped off Finn's words.

The men sized each other up, and Caitlyn couldn't help but do the same. She hadn't exactly forgotten Finn—how could she?—but reality was slapping her in the face now. Finn could give his leading men a run for their money when it came to heartthrob status. He had strong, aristocratic features made less harsh by a deep tan earned from his love of all things outdoors. His dark blond hair had sun-bleached lighter streaks, and, as always, it had that casual windblown look that all men who weren't Finn had to work hard to achieve. The dim light made it hard to see the color of his eyes, but she knew how their deep green could suck a girl in and melt her insides.

Finn had a good four inches in height on her admirer and, while both men were lean, he looked athletic and strong even in his suit. He might have the bluest of blue blood in his veins, but he had an edge that belied the DNA—not enough to make him look out of place in the throng of political and social elite inside, but it certainly set him apart.

It made the red-faced young man look ridiculous even trying to match up. He just fell short all the way around.

And his scowl was nothing compared to Finn's.

Which brought her nicely back to the real problem at hand. Finn had an odd gallant streak when it came to damsels in distress. At the right time it could be endearing—sweet, even—but this was not the right time for Finn to channel his inner caveman.

"I distinctly heard Cait tell you she was done talking. Do you really need to resort to assault?"

What's-his-name bristled visibly. Lord, the man was too

stupid to realize the danger lurking behind Finn's controlled cadence. *She* knew better, though, and launched into damage control before this got worse. "That was just a—"

"I know what that was, Cait," Finn snapped. He took her arm and moved her a few feet farther away, putting himself between her and the man like a bodyguard. He looked her up and down, then asked quietly, "Are you okay?"

"She's fine," the other man answered testily. "It's just a misunderstanding."

Finn's green eyes flicked in his direction. He obviously wasn't impressed with the man. "I didn't ask you."

He puffed up like a blowfish and Finn squared his shoulders. With all the testosterone in the air, this was about to get ugly.

Caitlyn cleared her throat. "I'm fine, Finn, thanks. And I would like us to all go our separate ways now so that this just remains between the three of us. There's a lot of press and a lot of people inside who don't need to be party to this."

Finn's eyes narrowed as he looked her over. "Are you sure?"

She nodded and saw Finn un-bow his shoulders a little bit as he released her arm. "Fine. No sense embarrassing you unnecessarily."

Thank goodness. "I'd appreciate that."

He turned to the other man, who seemed to get younger and weaker-looking as each second ticked by. "Go."

He shot them both a dirty look, then stalked away. She heard the noise of the crowd inside as the door opened, and then silence, blissful silence, broken only by the sound of the traffic on DuPont Circle, settled over the balcony again.

Caitlyn moved to sit on the bench against the balustrade and sighed as she pushed her hair back from her face. She needed a minute to get herself back together. First that guy, then Finn... It was all a little too much to process in such a short time.

"What the hell were you thinking, Cait?"

The heat in his voice hit her like a slap across the face. "Excuse me?"

Finn stood in front of her and crossed his arms over his chest. She could see the muscle in his jaw twitching. "What were you doing out here alone? Where's the damn security?"

How dare he jump on her over this? She gritted her teeth to hold her temper in check. "They're probably inside with everyone else—which is kind of the point, because I wanted a moment *alone*."

"Have you lost your mind? You don't get to decide to be 'alone' in a place like this."

"A place like this? It's a cocktail party, Finn, not a drug den. A 'place like this' should be the one place I *can* grab a minute to myself without worry."

Finn didn't seem to hear her. He was too busy glaring. "Then when some guy assaults you you try to arm wrestle him yourself instead of calling for help?"

"Like anyone would have heard me inside even if I did." Finn's eyes narrowed and the thin thread holding her temper snapped. Anger surged through her. "*I* didn't want to make a scene. And you'll please note I had the situation under control just fine before you even made your entrance." She lifted her chin. "If you want to play the hero, you might want to work on your timing."

He frowned. "You should know better."

"Why do you care?"

Finn's eyebrows went up, but before he could answer a door opened and three people came out to the balcony. They passed without speaking, but Caitlyn felt her face flush, anyway. She did *not* need to be seen in a shouting match with Finn. The list of things she didn't need was growing longer each day. Maybe signing on to this project wasn't the best idea, after all.

No. Folly *is perfect. It's a gift, so don't screw it up.* And, since Finn was running this project, she'd have to swallow her anger and pride and act like a professional.

Caitlyn forced herself to smile. "However, I appreciate your concern and will keep your warnings in mind for the future."

There. That was the proper thing to say to set the right tone for their future working relationship. She was pleased she'd made the effort. The look on Finn's face was just a bonus.

She thought he might be about to say something more, but Finn just shrugged, a signature movement showing that this was no longer worth his time. "So, who was that guy, anyway?"

She looked around. While more people had drifted onto the terrace, no one seemed to be paying them undue attention. She had to quit worrying so much about that. There was nothing attention-worthy about her and Finn speaking together. They had to: they were coworkers, colleagues working on *Folly.* There was nothing remotely scandalous about the two of them *talking.*

At a respectable distance from each other, of course.

"I don't know his name. All I really know is that he's a fan of the whole Reese clan and that he works for someone in Congress." The eyebrow that went up told her that Finn would be able to provide a name shortly, and she almost felt a touch of sympathy for the young man. "We spoke briefly inside. Obviously that wasn't enough for him."

"Obviously."

"I think he's had a couple of drinks, and we all do stupid things after we've had a couple of drinks, you know." Finn seemed to agree to that with a minuscule tilt of his head, and she blew out her breath in a long sigh.

"Are you sure you're all right?"

"I'm fine, Finn, really. It was a surprise, but that's all. I appreciate your rescue, but I doubt he would have pressed it much further. I probably just overreacted. Either way, I think I managed to convince him that I'm serious."

Finn chuckled and the sound rolled over her like a remembered caress. "If not, he's amazingly dense. Nice moves, by the way."

"Thanks. After that thing with Mom's stalker two years ago, she and Dad made me take some self-defense classes and work with a trainer. It's the first time I've ever had to put it to the test, though. Things were different in London. Fewer people knew who I was, so the weirdo potential was way down. It was a wake-up call I probably needed."

"Hell of a way to be welcomed home."

She swallowed as Finn came to sit next to her. There was still a respectable distance separating them, but that didn't stop her heart-rate from jumping up a notch. *Speaking of being welcomed home...* She'd thought about this moment a thousand times, planned a million witty and clever things to say that would put their past behind them, show she'd moved on and had her career firmly back on track. All those clever words eluded her now, damn it. But she had to say something or else look like an idiot.

She looked around, appreciating the dim quiet of the terrace and the view of D.C. beyond. A full moon topped the Washington Monument like a candle flame. "Beautiful view." *Well, that wasn't exactly inspired.*

Based on the slight twitch at the corner of his mouth, Finn agreed with that assessment. "Indeed."

"This is my first time in D.C., believe it or not. I'm hoping to have some time to do a little sightseeing."

"If you want tours of the Capitol or the White House let

Liz know. She can call my father's office and get it arranged for you."

She swallowed her shock. Finn rarely acknowledged his paternity, so the casual mention of Senator Marshall came straight from left field. Or maybe Finn and his father were on better terms now. Things could have changed. "I appreciate that."

This all seemed so normal. Two people sitting on a terrace, chatting. But it wasn't normal. This was *Finn*, and the proverbial gorilla sat between them, so the situation made her jumpy instead. Finn, though, seemed to be willing to ignore the past—or at least pretend that they were friendly strangers—so she was enough of an adult to do the same. If he wasn't going to bring it up, she should just thank her lucky stars and do the same.

"I didn't expect you to be here tonight." That was only partly true. She'd known there was a chance he'd be here; Dolfinn Pictures supported the summer camp program, after all. Because of that, the cast of *Folly* had come in an attempt to bring more attention to the fundraiser. But Finn normally avoided D.C. like the plague, *and* he'd been in Monaco for the last three weeks. Donor or not, the chances of him showing up had been slim. This kind of event wasn't Finn's idea of a good time. His scene was still more club than cocktail.

"Well, I have to put in an occasional appearance at things to keep the Grands happy."

Finn's grandmother sat on the board, and both she and her husband, the legendary Senator Marshall, were here tonight. Porter Marshall had held the office for decades before retiring and handing it over to his son, Finn's father.

The former senator was far more personable than Caitlyn had expected, and when she'd learned this evening that *The Folly of the Fury* was his favorite book, they'd had a lovely conversation about the importance of the book and character of Rebecca. Mrs. Marshall, though… *That* had been a slightly uncomfortable moment: although they'd never met at the time, Regina Marshall obviously recognized Caitlyn's name from before. While she hadn't been anything other than polite, Caitlyn had the sneaking feeling she was on probation with the regal matriarch of this powerful family.

Which was fine, because Caitlyn had no intention of screwing this up.

She had way too much on the line.

CHAPTER TWO

CAIT was acting strangely, which didn't make sense—or bode well for future work on *Folly*.

He'd sought her out tonight intentionally, wanting to get a clear-eyed assessment of who she was these days and whether or not she was going to make filming a personal hell for him. Dolby was the one who'd pointed him toward the terrace. The scene he'd walked in on, though...

He'd recognized the situation immediately for what it was, but hadn't known it was Cait until she'd had the man on his knees crying for mercy. He'd recognized her voice before the man even said her name—he'd had that irritated, clipped tone directed at him too many times to forget it. Then the details had hit him all at once: that coppery-blond hair that had kept hairdressers in business recreating the color on an entire generation of women, those long legs showcased by her signature stilettos, even the newly acquired curve of her hips that showed she wasn't starving herself anymore to fit the starlet mold.

The shock of seeing her had delayed his reaction time, and it had been over before he'd recovered. That was bad enough, but his *physical* reaction at seeing Cait again didn't sit well on top of everything else, and he'd let his anger loose on her. It was only his pride that had had him pulling it together to carry on a normal conversation.

Because he was not going to let Cait wreak her special blend of havoc on his life again. He'd learned his lesson there. He would keep this casual and professional if it killed him. He could be the bigger person.

"Are you ready to go back in?"

Cait seemed to be thinking very hard about a seemingly simple question. Finally, she shook her head. "Not just yet. I think I need another minute to cool down some and get myself together."

"It might have been fun to watch you break his fingers, though."

She seemed to consider that. "No. There are too many witnesses in there, too many cameras." She shrugged casually, but there was a wry smile of resignation on her face. "I don't need that kind of publicity this soon. Plus, it's tacky to start a fistfight at a cocktail party. Believe it or not, I *was* raised better than that."

At least her humor seemed to be returning. It was a long-standing joke between them: was the child of Hollywood royalty expected to behave better or worse than a child from political royalty? Using only the tabloids as their judge and jury, they'd never been able to come to a definitive answer as to how high or low the expectations really were.

And they'd certainly tested those expectations. Repeatedly.

He couldn't help but smile at the memory. "I could hit him for you."

She wrinkled her nose. "That's kind of you—and tempting—but I'm going to think positive thoughts that he's learned his lesson. The funny thing is that I think that might have been more about my folks than me. He seemed pretty interested in their political leanings and pet causes."

He understood now. Cait's connections—and all that Hollywood money—could be very valuable to an aspiring politician, and that guy had "congressional wannabe" written all over him. "Welcome back to the business."

She shot him a pissy look. "I never totally left, you know. Just because I haven't been working in Hollywood, it doesn't mean I haven't been working."

"On the *stage*. It's hardly the same thing."

Her eyes narrowed. "Don't start. I'm not going to get into that argument with you." She seemed to catch herself and her face cleared, and a wickedly innocent smile took the place of irritation. "But I'm rather flattered to hear that you've been keeping up with my career. That's rather sweet. I had no idea you cared."

Her tone rankled. There was no way he was going to let her go there. "Just because I wasn't consulted before you were brought on board, don't think for a second that I haven't verified you can actually pull this off. This film is my responsibility, and Rebecca falls outside *your* known range."

Cait's jaw tightened. *Oh, he'd hit a nerve with that one.*

She recovered quickly, though. She always did. She stood and stepped away from the bench before turning on him. "You know, if you spent more time actually working, and less time playing beach blanket bingo in Europe, you might not have to find out what's happening with your own projects after the fact."

The disdain in her voice chased off any desire he'd had to play nice. Where did Cait get off acting all high and mighty? "So you've been keeping up with my love life? That's kind of…sad, actually."

"Oh, please. Would you get over yourself? The last thing I care about is who you're sleeping with now. I'm here for one reason and one reason only. I want my career back."

He started to answer, but stopped short as a thought crystallized. Cait had been out of the spotlight for years; she wasn't exactly a hot commodity at the moment—famous parents or not. *Folly* was a great place to prove her skills, but it wouldn't do much to restore her to the fame and glory she'd once called her "birthright." Hadn't he and Dolby *just* discussed the headline possibilities today? A bad feeling crept over him. Maybe that was part of her plan. What better way to make the cover of every magazine and have her name on everyone's lips than to work that very Finn-and-Caitlyn angle he'd just laid plans to avoid.

"Oh, I don't know about that. It seems like a hell of a good way to make your comeback with a bang, doesn't it?"

He hadn't thought it would be possible for Cait to get any stiffer, but she did. With her arms crossed over her chest, she lifted her chin again until she was practically looking down her nose at him—something she could only do while he was seated.

"What *exactly* do you mean by that?"

"Being within fifty feet of me assures you every headline you want, doesn't it?" With a casualness he didn't really feel, but would grate on Cait's nerves regardless, he leaned back against the railing and stacked his hands behind his head. "Once upon a time, you claimed I was good for your Q Score. Looking for a second bite of the apple, Caity?"

Her eyes narrowed. "Your ego is simply unbelievable, Finn. Believe it or not, this is not about *you*. In fact, the very last thing I need—or want—is the kind of headlines you bring. I've grown up, worked damn hard to improve my craft *and* cleaned up my image. I take my job seriously." She eyed him with something he could only call distaste. "Since you can't say the same, why don't you just go back to Monaco until this is in the can? *That* would be very helpful for my comeback."

Oh, he'd definitely hit a nerve. Anger flushed her cheeks, and she gripped her tiny purse until her knuckles turned white.

"Now, if you'll excuse me, I have an early call in the

morning and should probably get some sleep." With that, she stalked away, head held high, and wrenched open the door to the ballroom to disappear inside.

Cait still liked to get the last word. Blaming him and storming off in a huff was her usual M.O., so that much hadn't changed. It was practically a repeat of that last night at his place. Everything had been his fault. Never hers.

He, however, had to think about bigger issues than Cait's temper. Too many people were involved in *Folly*. Money and reputations were at stake. And he would not let Granddad's glee at having *Folly* made be dampened by Cait and her possible dramatics. He would keep this project in line even if he had to kill people to get it done.

Finn gave himself a hard mental shake. He had to be rational about this. In the long run, Cait might prove to be a good choice for *Folly*. If she could pull off Rebecca, her name and potential star power could boost *Folly*'s box office revenues and award chances.

That didn't mean it was going to be less of a hellish mess in the meantime, though.

Caitlyn closed her door against the heat and spread her arms to embrace the icy chill of the air-conditioned trailer. Yesterday she'd neglected to crank the thermostat down before she left and had come back to a trailer almost as hot as the outdoors. But today... *Bliss, cool bliss.*

Her sweaty skin felt better almost immediately, and she peeled off the dress sticking to her back and hung it in the closet. Another thing she loved about this role: the fashions of the Forties were flattering and feminine and made it easy to really embrace Rebecca's character. In this heat, she was very glad *Folly* wasn't set in an era where she'd have to wear corsets and mountainous dresses. If so, she'd be battling heatstroke about now.

In just her underwear, she went to the fridge for a bottle of water. She left the door open while she took a drink, letting the cool air from inside wash over her.

She'd been in London too long, gotten used to what they amusingly called "summer" and forgotten how stinking hot and humid summer could really be in some parts of the country.

Walter Farrell had been an assistant director under her father for many years, and had learned his philosophy about authenticity from the master. Like her father, Walter felt being in a similar setting—like this insufferable heat and humidity—would help the actors really connect with the characters, but Cait was rapidly developing sympathy for all the actors who'd worked with her father. Especially on that one film set in the jungle...

But, honestly, she didn't care how much she sweated for this part. Caitlyn lay back on her small couch and fanned her face with her script. It wasn't false pride or inflated ego to say that this was possibly the best performance of her life. She was working with a stellar cast, Hollywood's best director—or at least second-best, she amended out of filial loyalty—and a crew that blew her away.

This was the life and the career she was supposed to have. It had just taken her a while to find the right path. She'd been given her second chance, and the only thing that really mattered was where she went from here.

She'd risk that heatstroke happily.

The only fly in her happy ointment was Finn. The rational pep talks she'd given herself about being an adult and leaving things in the past had turned to gibberish within just a few minutes of actually seeing him. It hadn't been her finest moment, that was for sure, but what had she really expected? The last time she'd seen him, she'd been hurt and angry, hurling ridiculous accusations at him because she hadn't been able to analyze, much less articulate, what she was really feeling.

She yawned and closed her eyes. Makeup had had a hard time covering the bags under her eyes this morning. She'd intended to call her mom today, but a nap seemed a more prudent use of her time since she still had several hours of filming to do tonight.

A 5:00 a.m. alarm was never fun, but she'd spent a good portion of the night staring at the ceiling as she tried to sort through the morass of conflicting emotions caused by seeing Finn. Of course the few hours she'd managed to finally sleep had been haunted by dreams that left her restless. Dreams of Finn.

Damn him for being so tactless. Why couldn't he be like normal people and politely ignore topics best left to die? Oh, no… He had to bring up personal junk in a professional situation.

And *that* was what she wanted to avoid at all costs. If she could, she'd give the entire planet amnesia so everyone would completely forget what had happened three years ago.

Too bad she couldn't give herself amnesia as well.

Good times, bad times… They weren't really classifiable as either. They were just "Finn Times"—fun and exciting at the time, but in retrospect not the wisest of choices and not an experience she'd like to repeat.

The residual tingle from last night's dreams rather belied those thoughts, but Caitlyn purposefully pushed those aside. Finn was tempting—very tempting—but she couldn't risk everything she'd worked for. *Eyes on the prize.*

But she would have to come to some kind of understanding with Finn. She'd accept her fair share of the blame, but that didn't mean she could just forgive and forget. Until last night she'd thought she was over it, but it hadn't taken long for all the old hurt to come rushing back.

Damn him.

She'd had more than her fair share of failed relationships—both before and after Finn—so why did Finn alone have the power to make her hurt?

Wallowing in the past would get her nowhere. She had to concentrate on now. Ignoring each other or acting hostile would be just as likely to attract attention and gossip. She could get through this...

A knock interrupted her drowsy thoughts. So much for that nap. She called, "Come in!" and reached for her water bottle.

"Stunning outfit, Cait."

Her eyes flew open in surprise, confirming that Finn was, indeed, in her trailer, and it took a second for the meaning of his words to actually register. Once they did... *Damn it.* Face hot, Caitlyn jumped up from the couch and grabbed the robe hanging on the bathroom door. Keeping her back to him, she shoved her arms through the sleeves. Granted, the old-fashioned underwear covered more than her bathing suit normally did, but that didn't change the fact she was wearing nothing but underwear and Finn was in her trailer. *Kill me now.*

She took extra time tying the belt to give herself a chance to regain her composure, but the chuckle coming from behind her didn't help. "I wasn't expecting you."

"I'm afraid to ask who you *were* expecting, then."

She refused to dignify that with a response. "Can I help you with something, Finn?"

"I thought we should talk." Finn dropped a stack of papers on the table before crossing to the fridge and looking inside. Her hackles went up at his nonchalant attitude.

"Fine. If you'll just wait outside, I'll get some clothes on—"

An eyebrow went up. "No need to be so modest, you know." *It's nothing I haven't seen before* hung in the air.

That knowledge didn't help her much at all. But then, Finn had probably seen so many women naked in his life maybe he'd have difficulty remembering exactly which bits were hers.

Not that she was having any trouble remembering *his*. Her skin heated. Oh, he was decently enough dressed today, in jeans and a simple black tee that fit snugly against his body, but memories of what lay under those clothes…

"Regardless, I'd rather you wait outside and we go somewhere to talk."

Finn pulled a bottle out and offered it to her. When she shook her head, he unscrewed the cap and took a long drink. Then he sat instead of leaving. She had to wonder if he was being difficult intentionally.

"Why can't we talk here? It's hot out there."

She pulled the robe tighter across her chest and wished it covered a bit more thigh. "I'd rather not."

Finn's exasperated look was almost funny. "What is *with* you, Caity?"

"Nothing. I just don't think it's a good idea for us to be seen meeting privately in my trailer. It's…inappropriate and might be misconstrued." *Ugh*, she sounded like a virgin schoolteacher.

Finn's look said the same thing. "You're not serious?"

"As you helpfully noted last night, my being within fifty feet of you will be enough to send the paparazzi into a frenzy. I'd rather not give them more to feed on." She went to the closet and grabbed jeans and tee shirt and waited for him to leave.

Finn ignored the hint, so she frowned at him to make her point. He gave her a look that questioned her mental stability instead, so she took her clothes to the bathroom and closed the door to get dressed.

"I'm afraid it won't take even that much," he called through the door.

"Exactly," she shouted back. "As soon as we're seen together—however innocent it may be—all those old, embarrassing pictures of us are going to resurface. I can't live all that down as old news if there's speculation there's new news."

Now decent, she came out and opened the shades on every window, giving anyone who walked by a clear view of what was going on inside. She'd have opened the door, but that would have just let the heat in. She wasn't willing to go that far. Propriety would just have to be served by open shades.

As she took her seat on the far side of the table, Finn snorted. "You're taking this a little far, don't you think?"

"I'm just cautious. You may not give a damn about appearances, but I do."

"How kind of you to worry about me." The smirk told her he was deliberately misinterpreting her words.

"Only to the extent that your reputation will impugn mine. I think we've proved that you can raise hell and people will still respect you, but I can't. It's a horrible double standard, so I've worked very, very hard to clean up my act." She picked up her water and drank deeply. After two disastrous starts, she really needed to bring her interactions with Finn back to the business they had in common. And *only* that. "So, what brings you by, Finn?"

He chuckled, and it put her on guard. "That very topic, actually."

"Your reputation?"

"Paparazzi, speculation, new news…"

That was odd. Those were the top three things Finn normally didn't even deign to give five minutes of his time to. He *really* didn't care about tabloid gossip.

A warning tingled up her spine, but she forced her face

to remain merely curious and clasped her hands together to keep them still. "Okay."

"After meeting with Dolby and Farrell this morning, we've decided to close the set for the rest of filming. Considering our past, they agreed it might be disruptive or distracting to have to worry about uncontrolled press for the next five weeks."

She held up a hand. "Wait." Barring any disasters, they'd be finished filming here by then. They shouldn't have to close the set permanently unless… *Damn.* She tried to keep her voice just this side of mildly curious. "You're not going back to L.A.?"

"No. Dolby will head back with the second unit tomorrow."

A headache began to form behind her right eye. "But why?"

"Because."

She waited for him to elaborate, but there was only silence. The man could be so unbelievably frustrating. She rubbed her temples. *Ugh.* "So you'll be here through the end?"

"Yep. Do you have a problem with that?" he challenged.

"No," she lied. She had a big problem with that. Multiple big problems. *You're an actress. You'll just have to* act *like it's not a problem.* "Do you?"

Finn looked completely unconcerned. In fact, he seemed to be biting back a smile. "Not at all."

"Okay, then." She took a deep breath. She, too, could play this game. "I'm glad you closed the set. I'd like to concentrate on my job. Not worrying about the press will make that easier. For all of us," she added.

"Unfortunately we're a little late for that."

That warning tingle took on an unpleasant sharp edge. As Finn pulled a couple of pieces of paper out of the stack and pushed them toward her, that edge cut deep into her skin.

Pictures printed from a blog. *Oh, no.* Caitlyn's stomach

sank. He first thought was that some blogger had already dug up old pictures of her dancing on tables and being carried out of bars by Finn. Or, even worse, that one picture of her and Finn on his motorcycle, her skirt hiked up too far and Finn's hand...

She didn't recognize the pictures, but the relief that flooded in was short-lived. There *had* been witnesses last night, after all. Damn. A picture of Finn and that guy staring each other down, another of her and Finn sitting on the bench, and another of her walking away, anger written across her face and irritation stamped on Finn's. She didn't need to read the accompanying text to add to the ill feeling rolling through her stomach.

"Already? Geez."

"I'd say welcome back, but—"

"I'd have to kill you if you did." Caitlyn took a deep breath and blew it out. "Are you sure you can't swap things around and go back to L.A.? Just let me get this film done without dealing with that kind of garbage?"

"No. And it would only postpone the inevitable, anyway." He looked at her oddly. "I mean, you *do* plan to move back to L.A. and start working again, right?"

"That's the plan. I'd hoped to have *Folly* under my belt, though, first. Something for people to talk about other than just my past."

His eyes widened. "So you really *don't* want that kind of publicity?"

Finally something she'd said was sinking in. "God, no."

"It made you a household name."

That reminder was unnecessary. She'd spent the last three years trying to change that association. "And it nearly destroyed me—personally as well as professionally."

Finn shook his head. "I don't think it was that bad."

The heat had made her grouchy, he'd given her a headache,

she hadn't slept well, and this entire day was now sucking with the strength of a black hole.

She lost her grip on her temper. "Well, you aren't widely known for your thinking skills, you know," she snapped.

Finn didn't bite back, and his cocky smile made her want to smack him. "Admit it. We had a good time."

Not even under the pain of torture would she admit that. It didn't matter now. She forced herself to keep her face neutral. "That was a long time ago. I'm not that girl anymore."

"What a pity." He smirked and took another drink.

Her jaw tightened so much it ached. *I will not take the bait. He's trying to get a rise out of me.* Why, she didn't quite know—other than his perverse sense of humor. She took a deep breath. "I guess I'll just solider through, then. You're right that I'll eventually have to face it, so I might as well start now." She rubbed her palms against her thighs. "You do your job and I'll do mine, and the ensuing boring lack of anything tabloid-worthy will set me up for a return to respectability. And when this film does well I should be solidly set."

"I watched yesterday's rushes. They're great. Really powerful stuff from you."

The compliment came out of nowhere, shocking her into silence while at the same time warming her. More than it really should. It made her slightly suspicious, too. Finn had always been quick with compliments on her appearance or a new dress, but never anything deeper.

"Thank you. Rebecca is a wonderful character. My mom even said she wishes she was thirty years younger so she could have read for the part."

Finn met her eyes over the table. "I can honestly say that, given the choice between you and your mother to be Rebecca, I'd choose you."

Shock and disbelief warred with a strange swelling in her chest. There was nothing he could have said that would have meant more to her, and she knew he knew it. The suspicion sharpened, but while Finn might be glib occasionally, he was also brutally, unflinchingly honest when it came to the business. The air felt weighty after his statement, and the silence between them was thick.

Caitlyn managed to find her breath and shrug casually. "But after Cindy Burke, of course."

Finn's lips twitched. Then, with a speed that had her rushing to catch up, he turned very businesslike. "There have been a few tweaks made to the schedule. As you know, we're a bit behind, and don't want this to drag on forever. There are some long days ahead."

She nodded.

"We'd also like for you to make a few more appearances to drum up publicity in the right places."

The cautious edge to his voice jerked her eyes to his. "With you?"

"God, no. I said the *right* places."

Caitlyn would have been relieved if not for the horror in Finn's voice. So much for any warm, fuzzy feelings he might have stirred up. Or any other equally warm, yet not at all fuzzy ones, either. She glanced at the list Finn passed her.

One name was conspicuously absent. "And Naomi?"

"Naomi has her own schedule and agenda."

She leaned back and sighed. This was juvenile high-school stuff on Naomi's part. "In other words she doesn't want to share her headlines. Especially with me. She never did."

"Naomi isn't stupid. She has a career to protect."

"Like I could do any damage to her. Like I ever *did*. The only person I dragged down was me."

"But you still managed to overshadow her."

"For all the wrong reasons, it seems." She shrugged. "But, you know, I crashed and burned, and she got what she wanted. I don't know why she carries a grudge."

That eyebrow went up again. "And you don't?"

There was more than one way to interpret that statement, and Caitlyn didn't want to get dragged back into a discussion of them. She chose to go with the subject of Naomi. "No. Naomi thinks this is a zero-sum game. She doesn't think there's room for us both in the papers. I know that's not the case."

A second, closer look at the schedule sent a chill down her spine. "What in the hell is *this* about?"

Finn shrugged. "The PR people want to shift attention from just you to you and Jason. Maybe get a couple of folks questioning whether you two are becoming a couple. It will shift focus nicely away from us." His lips twitched. "And a romance blooming on the set with your on-screen love is a perfect way to kill two birds."

Ugh. Was she destined to have to make a name for herself based on who she was—or supposedly was—dating? While Naomi got to keep the attention on the project and her role? It was degrading. It left a really bad taste in her mouth. "That's a cheap ploy."

If Finn didn't stop shrugging in that who-gives-a-damn? way she might strangle him. As it was, she was grinding her teeth into a pulp to keep from shouting at him to stop.

"But you know it works."

But Jason Elkins? He was a good actor—a big box-office draw—and they worked well together on camera but she didn't like him all that much. He was a little too egotistical and not exactly the brightest bulb in the chandelier.

She bit back each of the dozen comments she wanted to make about where they could stick this grand publicity plan. She had dues to pay again, and it seemed her penance wasn't quite over, after all. "Fine. I'm a team player. Whatever's best for the project."

"Smart girl."

She stood and reached for her shoes. "Don't patronize me, Finn."

"I wasn't."

He seemed sincere and Cait felt a bit bad. She was just too jumpy around him, ready to go straight to Worst Possible Meaning.

"Those were honest words from a friend."

Something icky rolled into her chest and brought a dull pain with it. Caitlyn chose her words carefully. "We were many things to each other, Finn, but I don't think we were ever really friends. Now we're colleagues, and there's no reason why we should be enemies, but I don't think we can be friends, either."

Finn's face was impassive, but she recognized the look in those green eyes. She hadn't hurt him with her words—past experience had proved he was impossible to hurt—but he was disappointed. Whether in her or her words or his own inability to charm her, she didn't know. She'd last seen that look three years ago as she'd walked out his door.

"I'm going to go get something to eat before I have to get back to Wardrobe. I'll see you around."

With that, she left him in her trailer and forced herself to walk calmly across the lot with a smile on her face. She even managed to make small talk with the crew as she grabbed a sandwich. She was proud of herself. Not for the way she'd left things with Finn—that had actually left a strange hollow feeling in her stomach—but for the fact she'd held her ground and set her boundaries.

But now that he wasn't right in front of her, all the old confusion and hurt—and, okay, she'd admit there was some residual desire and memories of good times and old feelings mixed in there as well—were rolling around inside.

So while she'd claimed hunger, she couldn't find her appetite.

As she sat in the makeup chair, she closed her eyes and tried to connect to the feelings so she could channel them into Rebecca later. When Martha started on her hair she opened her eyes and concentrated on acting as if everything was just fine. Normal. Same as yesterday.

Martha chatted and told jokes and Caitlyn laughed in all the right places.

Maybe she was a good actress, after all.

CHAPTER THREE

FINN didn't need to watch the filming—in fact, he probably shouldn't, since Farrell was notoriously temperamental and quick to bite when he felt his directorial turf was being trod on—but something drew him tonight whether he liked it or not.

Cait's parting shot bothered him. Oh, he'd been well aware before that she was carrying some kind of grudge against him—which was totally undeserved, because *he* wasn't the bastard in this situation. *He* wasn't the one who'd walked out.

So she wanted someone to blame? For what? *It nearly destroyed me—personally and professionally.* That did explain a lot of the shouting the night she'd left. He'd known she was starting to get a bit of backlash from their adventures, but "personal" hadn't come into it.

Or so he'd thought.

He'd chalked it up to overreaction from not getting the chance to read for that part she'd wanted in some film, and expected her to be back after she'd calmed down. The next thing he'd heard, she was in London.

She'd left the damn country without even saying goodbye. That still left a bad taste in his mouth.

London had changed her; she wasn't that fun-loving free spirit she'd been back then. She looked the same—he ignored the memory of the flash of heat that had moved over him when he'd walked into her trailer and found her dozing on the couch in just her underwear—but she wasn't the same. This new Cait was reserved, careful and locked down tighter than a maiden aunt—and equally disapproving. Every now and then she'd let something slip that made him think she was merely pretending to be someone new, but the mask always fell right back into place, making him wonder if he'd imagined it. What had happened to her in London to damp that inner fire that had once drawn him like a moth?

Not that he wanted to go there again.

Nonetheless, he was standing there watching, even when he had a ton of paperwork waiting for him. He could easily list a dozen things he *should* be doing instead of sitting here watching Cait prepare to make out with Jason Elkins.

His earlier compliment to Cait hadn't been empty flattery. In fact, he'd been astounded by how good she was as Rebecca. He snorted when he remembered that Cait's mother envied her the part. Even thirty years ago Margaret Fields-Reese would have been totally wrong for Rebecca, and if he wanted to be honest—privately, at least—Cait's mother couldn't have pulled it off at Cait's age. Cait might have spent the last ten years in the shadow of her parents' talent, but she was about to grab the spotlight all on her own.

That much he understood better than anyone else here, and he couldn't help but be proud of her.

Still, his brain had a hard time reconciling the Cait he knew and the roles she'd used to play with the woman now dominating each scene with quiet, heartbreaking strength. No wonder Naomi was spitting nails. Cait *owned* this film now. She would rule award season.

But even knowing Cait was simply in character, doing her job while the cameras rolled and thirty people watched, Finn was surprised at the strange kick that landed in his gut when Elkins kissed her.

And it only got worse when Cait kissed him back. The passionate embrace seemed to go on forever.

Farrell finally called cut and Cait rolled out from under Elkins immediately. Two women hurried over to fix her lipstick and hair while the crew readied for the next take.

"Not jealous, are you?" Dolby spoke from behind him.

That feeling wasn't jealousy. "Why would I be?" he asked casually.

"Don't know. All I *do* know is that the second he put his hands on Cait you looked like you would like to beat Elkins into a mushy pulp."

The truth was good enough here. "I just don't like him."

"Ah, but every woman between the ages of fifteen and fifty does."

And that equaled money at the box office. Finn shook his head. He knew all too well that personal likeability had nothing at all to do with job performance. Hell, his father was a prime example of a lousy person doing a good job, so his distaste of Elkins made little sense under close inspection. He'd had a lifetime of practice in keeping personal dislike separate from professional needs. It made things much easier. It took practice to keep everything in its proper box, but it worked well—until someone like Cait came along and screwed it all up.

As Brady would say, he needed to keep the bigger picture in focus. *Folly* was the important thing, and he needed to keep his focus there and there only. "I still don't like the idea of sending Cait out with him to bait the paparazzi. He's a womanizer."

"Bit of the pot calling the kettle black, I think."

For the second time in two days Finn really wanted to punch Dolby in the mouth. It was the only the third time in the entire seven years they'd been partners he'd been pushed like this, and Finn recalled Cait had been part of the reason that other time, too.

"The difference is that I actually like women. He's nothing but a user, and I feel like a pimp encouraging this."

Dolby raised his hands and stepped back. "Whoa, there, Lancelot. Lay off the talent. We need them. What did Caitlyn say when you told her?"

"That she's a team player. She'll do it, but I don't think she really likes the idea. I don't blame her."

"Well, she needs a big name in order to overshadow yours and point the cameras in another direction. Jason Elkins is about the only one who fits that bill. We could always go back to Plan A and put you two in front of the shutterbugs…"

"And I've already said that's not going to happen." Even if Cait were game, he certainly wasn't.

"You're so touchy about this. Three weeks ago you'd have let me sacrifice kittens on the set if it would be good for *Folly.*"

"Three weeks ago we were simply shooting. Now the entire project is just a backdrop for a freakin' soap opera."

"Dude, you need serious therapy."

Finn couldn't argue with that, but damned if he'd admit it.

The director called for quiet and cued the cameras. Cait lay beside Elkins, her face buried in his neck as her hand found his and their fingers twined together. It was beautiful, powerful…and completely sickening. Cait slowly sat up, her hair falling like a curtain over her face, and when she tossed it back the seductive smile she wore ripped into his stomach, spreading remembered and familiar heat and want through his veins. He recognized that smile, knew it, had had it directed at him when he… When they… Disgusted, Finn turned and walked away.

Dolby trotted beside him. Once they were safely out of

range, he spoke quietly, "If this thing with Cait is going to be a problem, I'll stay and you can go back to L.A."

Why wouldn't Dolby just let it go? Probably because he knew far more than Finn was really comfortable with at the moment. "There is no 'thing' with Cait, so there's no problem, either. I refuse to make a big deal out of this. The set is closed, Cait's going to go out and pretend to be hot for Jason Elkins and I'm going to produce this movie. If everyone will just do their damn jobs, it will all be fine."

Dolby threw up his hands in surrender. "Fine. *Folly* is all yours."

"How kind of you."

The assistant director waved them down and Dolby went to see what he needed. Finn went to the trailer housing the production office and tried to lose himself in the seemingly endless number of emails. About twenty minutes later, the subject line on one brought him up short: *Comment on Caitlyn Reese's return?*

Finn sighed. On the off-chance it was actually something worthwhile, he clicked it open. Nope. No questions about *Folly* or the role of Rebecca or anything else that might be considered anything other than tabloid-ready gossip.

Good Lord. When he'd left for Monaco, *Folly* had been newsworthy because of the importance of the project. The book had a nearly cult-like following, and was required reading at many universities, so film companies had been trying to buy the rights to the book for decades. Dolfinn's success had been hailed as the get of the year.

He wouldn't care if the attention shifted to one of the cast or the director, because that would be equally valid. In the last few days, as word had spread that not only had Cait been cast but that he would be on the set, *Folly*'s buzz had shifted toward the tawdry. The media was circling, but not in a good way.

He deleted the email without responding. The invasion of his private life didn't really bother him. Hell, he'd never had much of a private life. The Marshall family was always in the news: being rich and politically connected equaled fame, and he'd grown up in the fishbowl of power politics. It wasn't personal. And if it was personal, well, he'd learned long ago not to let that faze him.

He'd built his own reputation in L.A., proving that Marshall DNA wasn't destiny, but his connections and success only increased the glare of the spotlight. Honestly, he didn't care what was said about him; he lived his life exactly as he damn well pleased and the rest of the world could shove it. That was the one lesson he'd learned from his father that had served him well. Professional success came with personal scrutiny, but enough success meant his private life couldn't outshout it. Fame, fortune and power made him blog fodder, but they also meant he didn't have to answer to anyone about anything.

Why, then, did this sudden Cait-fueled interest irritate him? God knew there was nothing about their previous relationship that hadn't made the tabloids, and he'd never given that a second thought.

Until now. And he was finding out it was something he really didn't want to think about.

It made no sense at all.

"Beautiful, Caitlyn. Absolutely wonderful. You and Jason are just magic together."

Caitlyn accepted the compliments with a smile as she waited for the crew to reset the shot and the makeup artists swooped in to fix her hair and lipstick. She reached for a bottle of water and sipped gently through the straw. What she'd really like to do was swish and gargle to get the taste of Jason out of her mouth, but that probably wouldn't go over well.

She bit back a laugh. He looked good, smelled even better, and women everywhere would kill to be in her shoes right now. If only the teen magazines knew that their current cover hottie and winner of "Best Lips" should actually take home the title of "Worst Kisser." Not that a screen kiss would ever equal a real kiss, but jeez... There were close-ups involved, so chaste, fake kisses just wouldn't do. At their last rehearsal Walter had thundered on about authenticity and making it real, and she was really doing her best. If this was the best Jason could do... Well, Caitlyn felt a little bad for the women he dated.

Out of the corner of her eye, she saw Finn and froze. *What the hell?* It wasn't that he didn't belong here—he had full run of the set and there was a good chance he had a legitimate reason for observing the filming—but something slithered down her spine at the thought of him watching her do this.

It just seemed...*icky*. As if it was wrong somehow, even though she knew that was ridiculous. *They* weren't an item anymore, and this was professional kissing, not recreational. Then why did she suddenly feel like...?

The sound of her name pulled her out of her shock, and she realized the crew was waiting for her. Clearing her mind, she lay down next to Jason and let Walter direct her into place. She closed her eyes and took a deep breath, and at that moment she realized why Jason smelled so good.

That was the aftershave Finn used to wear.

Pieces fell into place and memories rushed back at her, crowding her mind's eye too quickly for her to focus on anything else. *Damn it. Now was not the time to wander down that path.* But as Jason's hands moved across her back it was all too easy to pretend it was just part of those memories. That those were Finn's hands touching her, his breath against her neck, his lips... A shiver ran over her body.

She sat up, pushing her hair out of her face, and when she

opened her eyes it was Finn's face she saw, his eyes hooded and glowing with desire. She let the memories wash over her and take control. Her fingers shook slightly as she reached for the buttons on her blouse, then a hand caught her hair and pulled her down against a broad chest. Only part of her mind registered the crew watching and the directions being quietly fed to her; something else was guiding her.

The word, "Cut!" finally caught her attention, and she snapped back to herself. The realization of who she was actually with sent heat to her cheeks, but she forced herself to keep her face still. Looking around, she saw the big smile on the director's face, and stunned looks from some of the crew.

Jason pushed himself to a sitting position and shook like a wet dog. Her lipstick stained his lips. "Wow, Caitlyn. Hell of a take."

Thank God this was a professional crew. They expected realism. She was the only one who needed to know what had actually happened, and as the compliments about that "magic" started again she didn't bother to correct anyone who wanted to gush about the chemistry she had with Jason.

That was way better than the truth. She felt as if she'd taken method acting to a whole different—and very disturbing—place. She felt shaken.

And something burned low in her stomach. One clear look at her co-star, though, assured her *he* certainly hadn't lit that fire. Caitlyn looked around surreptitiously, but Finn was gone. She couldn't decide it she was relieved or not. *That* had to have been one of her best performances, but maybe it was best he had not witnessed it. She wouldn't have been able to face him knowing…

And then she had to do it again. And again. Until finally—thankfully—she heard the true magic words letting her know they had everything they needed for this scene. She was done.

On slightly unsteady legs, she covered the distance to her

trailer in record time and collapsed on the couch. *That was weird.*

Even worse, something inside her had been released— as if the box she'd shoved everything Finn-related into had suddenly opened and, like Pandora, she couldn't get all the feelings back in. For years now she'd been able to disconnect from the past; the memories used to be like old silent movies, but now they came roaring back in a full Technicolor, surround-sound, 3D, hi-def experience. What had been just an old flame burning in her veins was now a brush fire fanned by all those old feelings.

And not all of them were good.

Finn wasn't good for her. Oh, he could be all kinds of fun—up for anything, unshockable, completely unconcerned about what the rest of the world thought. His "love-me-or-screw-you" philosophy had been just what she'd needed— then, at least. The acceptance had been what she'd needed.

Finn's attitude might come from a different place—in retrospect she could put enough pieces together to know some of it had been learned as simply self-preservation—but she'd still admired it back then. She'd needed it at the time.

But she wasn't Finn. She was living proof that his approach didn't work for everyone. Theoretically, it was a great idea. It didn't always translate well into real life. Regardless of anything else, she needed to keep that in mind.

So much for all those rational pep talks she'd given herself. *Ancient history. We're both adults. Time passes; people forget. No reason why we can't work together.* Lord, the platitudes sounded really weak now, and she realized they'd never actually been strong.

In her drive to move on and move ahead she'd let herself overlook one rather glaring flaw in her plan: Finn simply wasn't forgettable. Or ignorable.

But there was nothing that could be done now. Even if she

weren't contractually obligated to this film, she *wanted* this part, by God. Rebecca was more than just her ticket back to Hollywood; it was her chance to establish herself as a serious leading actress in her own right. No more playing the sidekick, always being compared to her mother and always coming up a bit short. She had a legacy to live up to.

Which meant she had to get all this Finn stuff under control.

And that seemed like a monumental task.

"Not hungry, Caitlyn?" Jason put down the paper he was reading and grabbed a strawberry off her plate. He smiled at her as he chewed, and Caitlyn could only imagine the caption that would go under the cute picture of him eating off her plate.

They were having a late, leisurely Saturday morning breakfast at a sidewalk café not far from her rented condo right off the water in downtown Baltimore. It was a trendy spot, carefully chosen to maximize exposure and photo ops for passersby. And it had worked; they'd drawn plenty of attention to themselves simply by doing nothing, and Jason's popularity ensured that those photos would make their way to the blogs in quick order. After three days of them filming love scenes, rumors were already rumbling about their "amazing chemistry" that "might mean something more." This breakfast would give those rumors legs, but only she knew the truth behind that so-called chemistry.

Jason reached for another strawberry without asking, and she pushed her plate across the table to him. "I don't really like to eat for the cameras. They always manage to catch me at just the wrong moment. I'll get something later."

He obviously thought that was funny, even as he chowed down on the rest of her fruit and yogurt, and while there was some truth to the statement, there were plenty of other issues complicating it.

Jason went back to his magazine as she stared at her paper, and to the world they'd look like any other couple having breakfast. She'd drawn a hard line about any snuggling or other public displays of affection, so they were going for the "comfortable companionship" vibe. Everyone would fill in all the blanks they wanted without Jason or her offering anything more.

She really hated this whole arrangement on principle. It was deceitful to pretend to a relationship—of any sort—simply to up her popularity by tying it to Jason's. She found it insulting on a professional level and personally distasteful.

At the same time it beat eating alone. Not by much, granted, but the grind of "work all day, go back to a rental alone at night" had started to lose its shine already. She didn't know anyone in Baltimore other than the cast and crew, and after keeping hours as long or longer than hers they weren't much for socializing, either.

She wasn't bored, but she was getting a little lonely. Jason was a poor substitute for actual company, but at least he was a breathing human being.

He'd been reading a magazine and now pushed it toward her. "Good interview."

"Thanks." At least that woman had given her the chance to put some of her past in a different, more flattering light. It was a start.

"This says you went to London and took acting classes."

"Yeah, I did some workshops, too."

"Rumor had it you went there to check into rehab."

She'd gone to London because it was far away from California and still in an English-speaking country. She'd considered Australia at first, but at least she knew a few people in London. She'd gone to hide and think.

"That's why they're called rumors. They're rarely true."

"Why?"

Jason was pleasant to look at, but talking to him made her head hurt. "Why what?"

"Why take classes?"

Was he really that slow? "To improve my craft."

"You already knew how to act."

"Yes, but there's always something new to learn, right?"

"If you say so."

And that explained so much about Jason. She'd now take bets that his career had an expiration date in the not too distant future. Caitlyn shook her head as Jason went back to his magazine. She'd had the talent and connections to get her start in the business, but she'd found out the hard way that it just wasn't enough.

She'd had plenty of time over the last few years to analyze how it had all happened and where it had all gone wrong, and the disturbing return of a whole bunch of feelings she didn't want to dissect didn't change any of her conclusions.

In many ways Finn had been the perfect choice for "Caitlyn Reese, Actress." He'd been a rising power player from an already powerful family, and his reputation and prestige were being bolstered by a string of successful films. She'd been the daughter of the industry's most respected director and America's favorite actress. Their relationship had given the papers great headlines—all kinds of garbage about the merging of dynasties.

While she had been born into Hollywood royalty, it wasn't really her world and she hadn't quite found her place. Oh, she'd had all the right connections to put her on a path to live up to her parents' legacy, but she'd never really managed to get all the pieces in the right places at the right times.

Growing up in that shadow had left her lacking certain social skills, and that had led to rumors of haughtiness and self-absorption, so that by the time she'd turned twenty-three she'd had a string of great acting credits to her name but no friends and little attention outside the films.

Then she'd met Finn. Their connection had been instantaneous, red-hot and immediately front page news. Overnight, her reputation had changed completely, launching her into the public eye like a publicist's dream.

Oh, she'd launched, all right. Right into the danger zone.

Finn had understood her—or so she'd thought. Being herself hadn't worked out all that well, and that had made the hurt worse. Then things had just gotten out of hand. It had been totally accidental, but that original plan had fallen by the wayside for her, and by the time she'd realized how deep in she'd gone, there'd been no graceful way out. Within six months she'd fallen just as fast as she'd risen, becoming a cautionary tale about the young, rich and famous in Hollywood. It had been utterly humiliating—for her and her parents.

But then she'd run away to London, and things had been different. Her reputation had preceded her, but without Finn to help fuel the fire she'd been able to live a bit more quietly. Distance had given her perspective, and after long discussions with her agent and her parents she'd launched her new plan. Her name guaranteed her acceptance into the right circles, but she'd never used it. Instead, she reinvented herself and thrown herself into acting classes and workshops. With the confidence she'd gained she'd made a new set of friends, and created a new life that was the polar opposite of the one she'd left behind. She'd taken smaller roles to stretch her range, gained some respect for those performances, then moved slowly up the ladder to bigger parts in the West End.

The constant exchange between the West End and Broadway meant she'd known plenty of people in New York when she'd arrived six months ago. Mentally, emotionally and professionally, she'd managed to end up in a good place.

A true redemption story, ready to be told.

But now… She was starting to feel a little restless and alone. The feeling was familiar, but not fun. And she could feel the pressure mounting already: she needed to be "out there," making the magazines, getting her name on people's lips again… Living up to her legacy.

Thankful for the sunglasses that hid her eyes, she glanced at Jason again. Yet, somehow she'd already been reduced to this.

Four more weeks. Only a month. She could handle it.

"You ready?" Jason's voice cut into her thoughts.

"Yes." *Finally*, she added to herself as Jason paid the bill and they left, setting off a new flurry of whispers when Jason put his hand on her lower back to guide her out.

Jason had left his car in front of Caitlyn's temporary home, and they walked the few blocks back. After they turned the first corner no one seemed to be paying any attention, and she felt her shoulders relax.

"I'm not really sure I like this idea of pretending we're something," Jason grumbled.

Surprise caused her to miss a curb and stumble a bit. Jason loved the attention from the press. Courted it, even. Maybe she'd pegged him wrong and he did have a conscience when it came to stuff like this. "Really? Me—"

The corners of his mouth pulled down as he shook his head. "You and Finn were high-profile. I don't want to look like I'm taking seconds or just your fall-back plan."

Her dislike of Jason grew a little more every day. "*Or* people might think that, given the choice between you or Finn, I chose you."

"I hadn't thought of that…" He brightened considerably. "I like that interpretation."

Of course you do. "Honestly, though, I don't want this to be any bigger than it has to be. I don't want anything coming back to bite me later, or anything that will look like we were intentionally trying to make people believe something false."

"But we are."

He just wasn't the sharpest knife in the drawer. "No, we're not. We're just not correcting their erroneous conclusions yet. We, as colleagues, had breakfast together. We might even catch dinner one night. People do it all the time, you know. I want to be able to honestly say we are just friends and make sure they'll have nothing solid to point to that might suggest otherwise."

"Then what's the point?"

She appealed to the one thing she knew would work: his ego. "You don't want Finn overshadowing you on *Folly*, do you? The producer shouldn't get more attention than the lead actor, right?"

"You're right."

"We're really just keeping attention where it belongs, instead of letting Finn run away with it."

"Good point." They paused in front of Jason's rental car. "Want a ride in?"

I've had about enough of you this morning. "Thanks, but I'll drive myself."

"See you later, then."

As Jason drove away she realized she was right, and that knowledge relieved her own conscience and brightened her outlook considerably. Not only would they keep the media's attention where it belonged—on *Folly*—they would keep hers there as well. Maybe this plan wasn't the worst idea, after all.

Provided it worked.

In the half-hour it took for her to drive from Baltimore to the set on the Patapso River, Caitlyn repeated every mantra and affirmation she could bring to mind so many times that she nearly believed the plan might actually work. Her mood began to lighten, only to crash when the very first person she ran into on the set was Finn.

Why was he hovering over the production like some first-timer who didn't trust the crew to do their jobs?

Finn looked mildly surprised to see her, but the explanation came quickly. "I thought you were having breakfast with Jason."

And good morning to you, too, Finn. There was an edge to his voice, though, that kept the retort behind her teeth. "I did."

Finn raised an eyebrow at her. "So where is he?"

That eyebrow grated across already raw nerves. "I wouldn't know. I'm not his keeper or his manager."

"But it went well?"

Define well. "The restaurant was lovely, and plenty of people saw us. That's what you wanted, right?"

"That was the plan."

This conversation was stilted, awkward and bordering on antagonistic. There was a set to Finn's jaw that she recognized as irritation held in check, but she couldn't be the cause. She'd just gotten here, for goodness' sake. She knew the root cause of *her* attitude, though, and while Finn was to blame, she knew it wasn't really his fault. She would just have to get hold of herself and get over it. And that would best be done at a safe distance from Finn Marshall.

"I'm sure Jason will be along shortly, and if I see him I'll let him know you're looking for him."

Finn shrugged. "Don't bother."

Okay, now I'm lost. "Then I'll just be in my trailer if anyone needs me." *Beating my head against the wall, trying to knock the stupid out.*

He nodded once, then walked away, leaving her standing there feeling rather foolish.

Once again, it was a feeling she was used to.

CHAPTER FOUR

EVEN though his body clock hadn't fully adjusted to the time change, Finn was up before sunrise Sunday morning—and sunrise was not something he saw very often. At least from *this* side. He often saw the sun coming up as he made his way to bed, and the fact he was up at such a ridiculous time only compounded his bad mood. He needed a good night's sleep.

Being back in his childhood room at Hill Chase normally caused him to sleep like the dead, but the dreams that had plagued him since Cait's sudden and unexpected return to his life still kept him tossing and turning all night. The strange sensation of want—rather like a nagging feeling—circling through his blood irritated him. Old flames had never held much interest for him before, but Cait seemed to be the exception to that rule, too. Hell, Cait had never run up against a rule she couldn't break, bend or circumvent. It was one of the things they'd had in common.

He'd finally given up all pretense of sleep and gone to the stables. A long ride on Duke helped clear his head, if nothing else. Although he was accepting of the changes that had happened in his absence, he still didn't really *like* what he was now in the middle of. His project was behind schedule, hovering dangerously close to going over budget... And then there was Cait. Oh, she was definitely a wrench in the gears he hadn't been expecting.

He should have sent Dolby to Monaco instead of risking *Folly* by going himself. He was paying for that bit of bad thinking now. Still, he had to admit that Cait was the right choice—even if it wasn't the choice he'd have made. *Folly* was better for having her in it, and he needed to remember this was about the project—not Cait, and certainly not him.

His sudden appreciation for rules and the need to keep the bigger picture in mind made him feel like he was channeling his brother Brady this morning, and that didn't help his mood, either. He needed to shake it all off and think about something else before he ruined his entire day.

He and Duke were already back in the stable before the hands had made their way in to start the day. Duke snorted as Finn handed him over to finish being brushed, and Finn gave him a treat before he left.

He missed Duke—and from what the hands said Duke missed him—but it wasn't as if he could move his horse to Malibu. But he really did need to start scheduling more trips home. And not just for his horse. The Grands weren't getting any younger. They were both still spry and in general good health, but for how much longer?

He and Dolby had toyed with the idea of expanding more into television, and with the number of shows shooting in New York, it would make sense to establish something on the east coast as well. New York was far enough away to keep him sane, but only a short train ride to D.C., and he could spend more time here to keep the Grands happy.

As Finn came up the hill to the house he could see the Grands on the back terrace, enjoying their morning coffee, which wasn't surprising. Granddad liked to watch the horses as they were turned out in the morning, as over the last few years he'd finally had to admit he was getting a little too old to be as hands-on as he'd used to be.

Yeah, after *Folly* wrapped he'd talk to Dolby about possibilities for Dolfinn on this side of the country.

"Good morning, dear. Did you enjoy your ride?" Nana waved him toward a chair, and he realized the table was already set for breakfast.

"I did. Let me wash up and I'll join you. I'm starving."

"Be quick," Granddad grumped. "Gloria's been holding breakfast until you got back."

"And bring the others with you," Nana called as Finn opened the door.

Finn stuck his head under the faucet and changed into clean clothes. As much as he would have liked to bang on Brady's and Ethan's doors, just for juvenile kicks, Ethan spoiled his fun by being in the hall already, still buttoning up a clean shirt.

"You were up early." Ethan's hair was still damp, meaning he hadn't been up very long at all.

"I don't have a lovely wife to keep me up all night."

Ethan's grin confirmed his late night, but before Finn could say anything, Lily came out of the bedroom, twisting her hair up into a ponytail as she walked. Lily's cheeks were flushed pink and she wore a small smile. *Seemed Ethan had been up for a while, after all.*

"'Morning, Finn."

"'Morning. They're waiting on us to eat."

Lily motioned them forward with a jerk of her head, since her hands were now busy tucking a tee shirt into her jeans. "Then let's hurry. I'm starving."

Finn smirked. "Can't imagine why."

Lily blushed even pinker. Ethan punched him in the arm and tried to frown him into good behavior.

A musical jingle floated from the other end of the hall, announcing Aspyn and Brady's appearance. Aspyn was a modern-day flower child, all the way down to the anklet of small gold bells that was the source of the sound. How she managed to tolerate his stick-in-the-mud oldest brother was a mystery for the ages.

Neither one of his sisters-in-law were anything like who he'd expected his brothers to marry, but he liked them both—sometimes more than his brothers.

"You were up at the crack of dawn this morning," Brady said. "Did you *have* to try to wake the whole house?"

Finn made a point of looking Brady up and down. "I obviously disturbed *your* beauty rest."

Aspyn shook her head at him in censure, but there was a small smile on her lips. "You're so bad, Finn Marshall."

He grinned at her. "Just part of my charm."

Aspyn laughed as she moved past all three of them and hooked an arm through Lily's. "Bloodshed before breakfast would make me lose my appetite. Let's go before they get too worked up."

Lily and Aspyn disappeared down the stairs, leaving him to the grumblings of his brothers. The smell of bacon grew stronger, and they arrived on the terrace just as Gloria and one of her many minions were bringing out a mountain of food.

Ethan surveyed the table. "All of Finn's favorites again, I see."

Gloria swatted Ethan and leaned in to kiss Finn's head as if he was still a child. Last night's menu had been one of his top five favorites, too. He hadn't eaten that well in months.

"You, Ethan Marshall, are out here all the time, eating your way through my kitchen like a teenage locust. I don't get to cook for Finn very often."

"I'd consider that a blessing," Ethan grumbled as he pulled out a chair for Lily.

Aspyn took a seat across from him, leaving Finn trapped between Ethan and Brady.

"Just eat," Gloria scolded. "Especially you, Lily. Aspyn, that sausage is the vegetarian type you like." Gloria fussed around the table for a minute more, then patted Finn fondly before she returned to the kitchen.

"See, it's true that absence makes the heart fonder." Finn loaded up his plate with Gloria's famous French toast—so famous that the White House chef had asked for the recipe and been politely turned down. "That and an autographed picture of Pierce Brosnan gets me French toast today."

Ethan dumped a pile of bacon on Lily's plate before filling his own. Lily slid half of it back onto the platter. "I guess we're lucky she didn't kill the fatted calf," he muttered.

"Maybe that's dinner tonight," Granddad offered.

"Alas, I can't stay. I'll be leaving right after breakfast." Nana started to protest, but Finn shook his head. "I'm sorry, Nana, but I'm just covered up with work. I'll be back next weekend, I promise. And once we wrap I'll come stay for several days before I head home."

"This is also your home," Nana said pointedly.

Guilt swamped over him, just as he knew she'd intended. "I know."

Brady sipped at his coffee. "Some prodigal son you are, coming home and immediately leaving."

"You should really brush up on your allegories before you try to drop them into conversations. Prodigal would imply I'm coming home broke or in disgrace, and I'm neither, thank you very much."

Ethan leaned close. "Nor looking to reconcile with Daddy," he muttered under his breath.

Finn snorted, Ethan jumped as Brady kicked him under the table and Nana frowned at them all. Her tone cool, she said, "That much is true for the time being. It would be nice to keep it that way."

Finn knew she wasn't addressing Ethan's crack about their

father. She understood that minefield too well to go there. They would all just pretend nothing had been said at all. That was the Marshall family plan. Ignore everything you can.

"Believe me, Nana, I've got plenty of money. Ethan can vouch for me on that."

Her eyes narrowed. "That's not what I was referring to, and you know it. I'm very tired of seeing your name in the paper for all the wrong reasons."

A smart remark about not reading the papers sat on the tip of his tongue, but Finn held it back. He had no such reservations when it came to Ethan and Lily, both of whom were fighting back smiles and looking ridiculously innocent. "Oh, like you two have any room to talk."

"Ethan is one hundred percent reformed." Lily somehow managed to sound prim. "And I'm the freakin' poster child for reformation."

"There's nothing worse than a former sinner to lay on the condemnation."

Lily merely smirked at him. Ethan was obviously a bad influence on her.

"The point, Finn, is that eventually everyone must grow up and settle down." Nana leveled a look at him. "You're almost thirty. Don't you think it's time?"

Finn looked to his grandfather for help, but Granddad feigned interest in his breakfast. Brady wore his usual smug smile, and Aspyn examined the hem of her napkin. But Lily and Ethan, those traitors, were nodding in agreement, egging Nana on. Not that she needed help at any time, but after marrying off both of his brothers in a little over a year, Nana was looking for the hat trick.

Finn leaned back in his chair and glared at his brothers. "Really? You want to go there?"

They both just lifted their left hands to show wedding bands.

"Nice try. But neither one of you got anywhere close to an altar before your thirtieth birthdays, so I figure I still have a little time."

"You're missing the point, dear. While I—and your grand-father—" she waited for Granddad to nod his agreement "—would love to see you settled and happy with a nice girl one day, I'm more concerned with the situation currently at hand."

Oh, please don't go there. I'm not in the mood. "And that would be…?" he asked innocently.

"Caitlyn Reese."

Yep, she had. Nana had a knack for going right where he didn't want her to—and she could make him feel twelve years old again at the same time. Defensive maneuvers would only play right into her trap. And this was Nana, so offensive ma-neuvers weren't allowed at all. Playing dumb seemed his best bet. "What about Cait?"

The irritated lift of her eyebrow clearly stated she wasn't buying his dumb act. And a quick look told him that Lily and Aspyn had joined Granddad in his studious approach to eating, leaving Ethan and Brady watching avidly with get-yourself-out-of-this-one smirks on their faces. He couldn't look there for help, but maybe they wouldn't be a hindrance, either.

He could hope. But he wouldn't hold his breath.

Nana set down her fork and met his eyes evenly. "I met Miss Reese the other night at the benefit. She's not at all what I expected based on her previous behavior with you."

"We were young and just having a good time. So we made the tabloids. It's not like I'm the first Marshall to steal a head-line. It's practically a rite of passage in this family."

Brady cleared his throat. "It was more than just one head-line. You two tore a swath through southern California. *We* remember those days clearly, even if they're a vodka-soaked blur to you."

Oh, his memories were just fine. Working overtime, in fact.

He looked to Lily, who merely shrugged, then to Aspyn, whose nose was wrinkled slightly in apology.

"Even I remember them, Finn, and I spent most of that summer chained to a tree in Oregon."

Brady turned to Aspyn. *"What?"*

"Nothing. More coffee?" Aspyn smiled angelically at Brady's we'll-talk-about-this-later scowl. "All I'm saying, Finn, is that you two were news, and no one has forgotten it. Caitlyn may have been more low-profile the last few years, but you haven't. I saw an interview with Caitlyn's mother recently, and she's very excited about her daughter's return to their family business. Put all of that together, and you've got people's attention whether you like it or not."

"Exactly," Nana added. "Regardless of your past deplorable behavior, Miss Reese seemed to be a lovely and quite charming young woman. And from what I hear she's showing signs of reformation as well."

There was a bear trap here, waiting to snap on his foot, but damned if he could tell exactly where. "I'll tell her you said so."

"I'd like to have the same things said about you. You've already made the papers..."

"It's nothing, Nana. You know how these things go. Rest assured that I have no interest in Cait beyond her performance. This is strictly professional. In fact..." He could not believe he was saying this. "Rumor has it that Cait and Jason Elkins might be becoming more than just co-stars."

"I'm glad to hear it, and I wish them well." Nana picked her fork up again. "I'm sorry to have brought up such an unpleasant topic at the table, but I'm happy that we got it sorted out."

"Nice save," Ethan whispered behind his coffee cup. "You almost had me believing it."

"Shut up before I make Lily a lovely young widow."

Nana cleared her throat. "We're old, not deaf, you know."

Lily snickered, which earned her a grin from Ethan, but Finn could only frown at her in retaliation. So he kicked Ethan under the table instead, earning him a "what did I do?" look.

Granddad, thankfully, changed the subject. "How's my movie coming along?"

"Fantastic." Finn liked the way Granddad smiled when he spoke about "his" movie. The first Senator Marshall had been the subject of a bio-pic about his career and characters in movies about the civil rights movement and the war on terror. He'd even played himself in a comedy set in the Capitol. But *Folly* was the movie Granddad considered "his," and that pushed Finn to put up with whatever he had to in order to make it happen.

It was because of Granddad that Finn had even gone after the rights, and it was Granddad who'd finally been able to convince the heirs to agree to sell. It turned out that the author had been a supporter of Granddad's career. *Folly* was Finn's present to the man who was more his father than his grandfather, and he'd even gone as far as to cast his brothers and cousins in small cameos as an extra treat—but Granddad didn't know that.

"Are you sure you don't want to come to the set and watch? Maybe be an extra?"

"No, no. I don't want to ruin the experience by knowing what went into it. I expect excellent seats at the premiere, though."

"Done."

With that assurance, Granddad stood and extended a

hand to Nana, and they left for their morning walk over the grounds.

Lily sighed as they walked down the path. "Your grandparents are like characters from their own romantic movie."

Finn looked at her over his coffee. "Still reading those romance novels, Lily?"

Lily lifted her chin proudly. "Every chance I get. I believe in happy endings. Your Grands, Brady and Aspyn…" Lily paused to accept Aspyn's nod of agreement before smiling adoringly at his brother, who grinned back like a lovesick teenager. "Ethan and me."

"Spare me the details, please. I just ate."

Lily grinned as she pushed her chair back from the table and stood. She kissed Ethan, and then leaned down close to Finn's ear. "Your day will come, Finn Marshall," she whispered.

"Is that a threat?" He heard Brady's snort and Ethan's chuckle.

Lily shook her head. "Just faith in your happy ending. You deserve one, too." She winked before she straightened up and turned to Aspyn. "I'm going to the stable. Want to come?"

Aspyn nodded and stood. "I'm with Lily on this one— literally as well as metaphorically."

With that, both women walked away, the sound of Aspyn's anklet jingling along with Lily's laughter. That left him with only his brothers at the table, and both of them were staring at him. "What?" he finally asked when the silence got too long.

"She's not wrong, you know."

Of course Ethan would agree with his wife. "That my day will come?"

"That you deserve a happy ending."

Finn looked at Ethan carefully, but couldn't find any trace

of sarcasm. "Not you, too? I get enough of that from Nana. Just because you—"

"This has nothing to do with me."

"Or me," Brady added.

"Or even Nana's quest to get you to the altar," Ethan said.

"Then what *is* this about?"

Ethan cleared his throat and looked slightly uncomfortable. Brady sat silently and Finn knew he was about to hear something he wouldn't like.

"At the risk of sounding like your therapist—"

He was right. "I don't need a therapist."

Brady coughed. "Maybe you should reconsider that stance."

He leveled a stare at both of them. "Because…?"

Ethan snorted, sounding so much like Brady that Finn did a double-take. "The one relationship you've had with a woman that lasted longer than six weeks was with someone even more screwed up than you."

The anger that flared on Cait's behalf startled him. "Don't—"

Brady stopped him. "There's no need to jump to her defense. I'm sure she's got many fine qualities, but you two took hedonism to new extremes, and it doesn't take a shrink to see that you simply fed off each other's demons."

If anything, they'd been exorcising them. "I don't know what the hell you are talking about."

"Don't you?" Brady's eyebrow went up. "Caitlyn's background is oddly similar to yours—a famous family, the constant scrutiny by the press, the pressure of expectations. You seemed to find the one person on earth who was equally as emotionally disconnected as you—and you couldn't even make *that* work."

"Cait and I were just having a good time."

Brady lifted his coffee mug in a mock toast. "And you just proved my point."

"You had a point?"

"You barely let us—your family—into your life. You certainly don't let anyone else in. It's all superficial and safe. Easy, even. I know how attractive that feeling can be. But it's dangerous. If you can't find someone else to care about, you end up caring only about yourself. And then you're no better than our father."

"That is ridiculous."

Ethan took the opportunity to pile on. "We have always backed your decision to move to California. We, more than anyone, understood your need to get the hell out of Dodge. You were so young when Mom died. It was much harder on you, because you didn't know what an ass he was before then. Things were so screwed up after that I'm surprised you didn't end up in therapy."

The jump from Cait to his father had Finn struggling to keep up. "You think I have daddy issues? Me and half the world. The man's a royal bastard, but I'm hardly scarred by it."

"Aren't you?" Ethan asked.

Before he could do more than shake his head Brady added, "Why do you think the Grands ride you so hard? They see the signs, the pattern re-emerging."

That cut disturbingly close to the bone for Finn, but Brady wasn't done.

"Do you think they're proud of the kind of son they raised? The man he is today?"

"He's a senator, for God's sake—and a good one, too. Most parents would be pretty pleased."

Ethan waved that away. "Professional success isn't the same thing. You have that already and they're proud. Disgustingly so, if you ask me. But still they worry."

This conversation had hit too many sore spots, and Finn wanted out. "Then find them something else to worry about." He turned to Ethan. "I know—why don't you get Lily pregnant? That should distract them nicely."

Ethan smirked. "Done. But it's really too early to be telling folks."

Finn choked on his coffee and it burned all the way down. "Seriously?" At Ethan's nod, he looked at Brady, who showed no surprise on his face. It must be true, and Brady must have known already. "Congratulations. When?"

"About seven months. But we're not changing the subject just yet. Back to Caitlyn—"

Cait wasn't exactly a change of subject, but it beat their armchair therapy hands-down. "I have no interest in Cait beyond her performance in *Folly*. And it's award-worthy, by the way."

"I don't doubt it. Lily and I saw her in London about eight months ago. She made a wonderful Desdemona."

"Her acting ability has improved dramatically, pardon the pun."

"And that's your only interest in Cait?"

Finn nodded.

"Then have a little pity on the poor girl," Brady said. "Haven't you caused her enough trouble?"

Damn it, he was *not* the villain in this. In any of it. Not now and not then. Cait was not some poor, naïve girl he'd led astray. "Cait grew up in the tabloids, and she understands this business better than you think. If she didn't want to be in the headlines again she wouldn't have signed on to one of my projects."

Brady shook his head. "Make up your mind, Finn. Either it's something or it's nothing."

"It's nothing that's anything for you to worry about."

Ethan turned to Brady. "Twenty bucks says it's something."

"There's no way I'm going to take that bet. We both know it's something. My only question is how much of a something it's going to be."

This was one of the many reasons he spent his life on the opposite side of the country from his family. No one should have to put up with this level of interference. "I'm going to say this one last time, so pay attention. Regardless of what Cait and I used to be, our relationship now is strictly professional." His strange reaction to seeing Cait kiss Jason niggled at him, but he pushed it aside.

That statement got him disbelieving snorts from both brothers.

"Then you're stronger than I gave you credit for. Either that or you're an idiot," Ethan clarified.

He'd kill Ethan, but the Grands would disapprove. They seemed to actually like him for some reason. "Speaking of idiots, you and Lily are due on the set Friday by two for Wardrobe and Makeup."

Ethan and Brady exchanged a look that told him they were dropping the topic, but Finn knew it was probably only temporary. Their matching smirks confirmed it, but Finn would take what he could get at the moment. All this talk of Cait had churned up too much history, and he didn't need that today.

Ethan's smirk transformed to a grin. "Oh, I'm really looking forward to it."

He sounded far too cheerful and sincere for someone who'd grumbled about it from day one. Finn was instantly suspicious. "Why?"

"Because who can resist watching a slow-motion train wreck?"

Brady nodded. "When are Aspyn and I scheduled again? I can't wait."

With a glare that only caused his idiot brothers to laugh, Finn stood and tossed his napkin on the table. He didn't bother to comment as he walked away, leaving them laughing like loons behind him.

Had he really been considering a move back to this side of the continent? Where he could have this kind of conversation on a regular basis?

Yeah, New York was going to be too close as well.

CHAPTER FIVE

ALTHOUGH the set was officially closed to the media at large, they simply couldn't afford to keep all the press away. Interviews had to be done; the project had to be pimped properly. So, while she'd much rather go back to her trailer for a rest from the heat and a little peace and quiet, Caitlyn put her game face on and smiled back at the over-excited reporter from *Insider Unlimited*.

The first few questions were the usual—what was it like to be back? How excited was she to be a part of *Folly*?—and Caitlyn fell back on stock answers to save her energy for the questions to come. And they did.

"So, Caitlyn…" The I'm-your-best-girlfriend tone was a dead giveaway that the next question was a zinger. "We've heard there's some tension on the set between you and Naomi Harte."

"There's always tension in any production," she interrupted with an airy wave of her hand. "We're all working very hard, very long hours, and it's really hot this summer. It makes us all grouchy." She kept her voice light. "The relationship between Angela and Rebecca is very complex and emotional, and maybe folks confused on-camera tension with real life. All I can say is that Naomi is perfect for the role of Angela, and it's wonderful to be working with her again."

The plastic smile of the reporter faltered for a moment,

but then she narrowed in. "Three years ago you had a very public and *dramatic* relationship with Finn Marshall. Does it make things awkward now?"

She'd prepared herself for this, practicing low-key answers that couldn't be misquoted out of context. "Only in that I never knew how hard-working Finn really is, and how much he cares about this project. As a producer, he has the Herculean task of making things happen. Keeping a production of this size and complexity running smoothly is much harder than people think. I never had the opportunity to work with him before now, and I'm just blown away that he's *that* good at what he does." *There—that should shut her up for a bit.*

"So there's no problem?"

"None," she lied with a shrug.

"And the rumors about you and your co-star Jason Elkins?"

She'd practiced this, too, and she knew her smile was the perfect mix of humor and censure. She'd learned the art of this dodge from Mom, the true master of misdirecting the press. "Are probably greatly exaggerated. We *are* spending a lot of time together, but that's the great part about liking and respecting your coworkers. You have someone fun to hang out with after work."

Whether it was from disappointment that Caitlyn wasn't giving the answers she wanted or something else, the reporter wrapped up quickly after that and thanked Caitlyn before moving on to her next interview.

Proud of the way she'd handled that, Caitlyn sipped at her water and pulled out her phone while she could still ride on that high.

Her mother answered on the third ring. "Caity, darling! How are you?"

Where to begin? She couldn't exactly tell her mother that she was caught in a melodrama that had nothing to do with the script. Not when Mom had taken her at her word that this time would be different. Without embarrassment to the Reese legacy.

"I'm okay," she hedged. "Just had a few minutes and thought I'd say hi."

"I only have a couple of minutes myself. We are actually about to board a plane for Spain."

Of course. "I forgot about that. Daddy's getting some award, isn't he?"

"Lifetime Achievement. And he sends love."

"Love back to him. I guess we'll talk when you get back."

"Is everything okay there?"

"Yeah, of course. We're a little behind schedule, but…"

"Oh, it's so annoying when that happens. You should—"

Caitlyn could hear her father in the background, hurrying Mom along.

"Look, darling, I've got to go. You know how John is. I'd tell you to be wonderful, but I know you will be. I'll call when I get a free minute tomorrow."

"Okay. Bye," she said, but the line was already dead, and she knew that "tomorrow" really meant sometime next week, when her mother remembered her again.

Caitlyn felt slightly deflated, but not surprised. Her parents were always on the move, always had been, and she was quite used to it. It came with the territory. Hell, she'd gone through this very issue with her therapist a dozen times as a child, and the mantras came back easily. John and Margaret Reese didn't belong to her; they belonged to everyone. That didn't mean they didn't love her, but they had careers that demanded so much of them she had to adjust *her* demands and expectations.

Maybe it was for the best. There was no reason to dump her problems at their feet. It wasn't as if they could do anything. She'd handle this the way she handled everything else, and if she needed advice she'd call her agent.

They'd be at the premiere, though. They never missed one of those. When she felt cynical she credited the photo op, but she knew they came because they were proud of her. And they'd be even more so when they saw *Folly*. Mom wasn't the only one a little envious right now; Daddy had gotten his nose a little out of joint at hearing one of his protégés would be directing. He'd been after *Folly*'s rights for years.

Everything would be fine in the end.

But first she had to get through filming without having the whole thing drive her over the edge. She felt jumpy and tense, and no amount of meditation could help alleviate the stress of navigating this minefield. A strong drink sounded grand.

Taking a deep breath, she headed back to Wardrobe, past where the reporter was now interviewing Naomi with over-the-top gushing. Caitlyn maneuvered behind her cameraman just in time to hear the reporter say, "So, has there been any tension between you and Caitlyn Reese over your new romance with Finn Marshall?"

Caitlyn stumbled, and Naomi shot her a sly smile before turning back to the camera.

But she couldn't hear Naomi's response over the roar in her ears.

She managed to avoid Finn for the next week. Well, mostly. It was impossible to completely avoid him on set, but she kept those interactions quick and tried to include an audience whenever possible. That audience and her determination to focus solely on business didn't stop Finn from making inside jokes that had her gritting her teeth, but it helped her hold her tongue and not say anything she'd regret.

While she could physically avoid him as much as possible,

mentally Finn was constantly bothering her. She'd gotten to the point where she couldn't film a romantic scene with Jason *without* picturing Finn the whole time. Method acting had taken on a whole new meaning in her life, and she wished she'd never even heard of it.

Most of her scenes in the film ran parallel to Naomi's, but the ones they did have together had taken on a sharp edge that the director loved. And, again, that came from Finn. Their characters were supposed to be at odds over Jason's character, but the real-life idea of Naomi and Finn added extra bite in their performances. Caitlyn told herself that Finn wasn't her business, but the fact it was Naomi of all people just rubbed her the wrong way.

Thankfully, she didn't have to witness any nuzzling or snuggling on the set—they were both too professional for that—but the papers were full of Naomi and Finn having a quiet dinner or seeing a movie. Even Jason started to get a little annoyed—he didn't mind sharing the headlines with Naomi, but Finn taking those headlines was just too much for his ego. *Their* "quiet dinner" hadn't garnered nearly as much attention as Finn and Naomi's. Tempers were running high all over the place, and the heat didn't have much to do with it.

Caitlyn felt as if she was living in the middle of a melodrama. Her countdown of days left on the set was all that kept her sane. It would all be worth it soon enough. She could do this.

Of course just as Caitlyn almost had herself believing this little pep talk, the whole plan had to go to hell.

Chris, the assistant director, was a native New Yorker, and had joined her today at a table in the shade for a snack. Their conversation had turned into a debate over the best place to get Korean barbecue in the city. She had just elicited a promise from him to at least try her favorite place before he recommitted to his earlier choice when he suddenly looked up and shouted Finn's name.

"Sorry, Caitlyn, but I've been trying to track him down all day. It won't take a minute."

That gave her a whole five seconds to steel herself before Finn sat down across from her. "Hi, Finn. If you two need to talk, I'll go."

Finn gave her a strange look that said he was well aware she was trying to avoid him as he returned the greeting. She made to leave.

"No, don't," Chris said. "You're not finished eating, and it's not like we have something top secret to discuss."

Put like that, she didn't have any reason *not* to sit there while Chris and Finn went over something about the schedule. She checked her phone for messages, sent an email to her parents and quietly looked up her name on Google to see if anything had made the blogs.

She heard, "See you later, Caitlyn," and looked up to see Chris leaving, already involved in a conversation on his own phone. That left Finn at the table with her, and awkwardness settled in quickly.

For her, at least. Awkwardness of any sort just wasn't in Finn's repertoire of emotions. He seemed totally at ease. Casually dressed in a tee shirt and jeans, he looked ready to step into a music video, while she felt wrung-out and haggard and in desperate need of a trip to Makeup. And while it was comfortable enough here in the shade, and a nice breeze had finally kicked up, his hairline was damp, as if he'd been doing something in the sun to work up a sweat. The entire effect was one of ease and confidence. *How did he manage that?* It just wasn't fair. She just felt wilted.

"So how are you, Cait? I haven't see you in a few days." He picked up his sandwich and took a bite. Now she really was stuck. There was no way she could walk off and leave him to eat alone—especially since she knew how much *she* hated to do exactly that.

Breathe. "Good. And you?"

He shrugged. "You and Jason got the cover of *Star Track* this week."

As did you and Naomi. Pride kept her from saying anything, though. "That's what you wanted, right?"

Finn's over-dramatic sigh was almost funny. "*I* wanted a shoot uncomplicated by outside problems. A media circus— regardless of the cause—only makes my job harder."

Since Finn was dating his talent rather publically, that rang a little false. "Jason and I were *your* brilliant idea."

Finn shook his head as he swallowed. "Actually, it was Dolby's."

"Whatever. Whoever was responsible for starting the whispers did a good job. You'll notice those pictures are completely innocent until a heavy layer of speculation is applied."

An eyebrow went up. "So it *is* all just a rumor?"

She nearly choked. "Of course it is. How can you even ask that?"

"I've seen your love scenes." He smirked and she wanted to kick him under the table. "They're hot. And emotional."

Caitlyn felt the blood rush to her face. She hoped he'd think it was from the compliment he'd just paid her. The truth would go with her to her grave. "Thank you."

"I can see how folks might think—"

"But *you* should know better. Anyway, only people who have never tried to kiss someone when there are dozens of people watching and there's a camera ten inches from your face would ever think anything like that. It's far from romantic."

"So how do you do it?"

Finally her chance to give him a little bit of that mock back. "It's called acting. I'm sure you're familiar with the concept."

That earned her a frown. "I meant you, specifically."

"Why?" she knew she sounded suspicious and defensive, but she couldn't help it.

Surprise crossed his face. "Because I'm interested in craft."

It was her turn to be surprised. "Since when?" Never once had they talked about craft. Or business, either.

He shrugged again. It pushed her over the edge. "*Please* stop doing that."

"What?"

"Shrugging. Don't ask a question and then pretend the answer doesn't matter. Either you care about something or you don't."

"That's a lot to read into one shrug."

Only because she had a history with that shrug. It practically defined everything that had been wrong with their entire relationship. Not that she was going to tell him that. "Lesson one on craft, then. Body language matters. It doesn't matter what comes out of your mouth or what you meant. What people perceive is what they believe. And that's just as true on-screen as off."

"You sound awfully bitter about something."

"I have cause to be, don't you think? I learned that lesson the hard way."

"Poor Cait."

She would *not* let him rile her. "The fast trip from rising star to cautionary tale is fueled solely by what people perceive about what they see."

"It wasn't that bad."

"Please. The only thing that kept me from being blackballed in the industry was my parents. That and the public's never-ending interest in watching a train wreck."

"You're exaggerating. I was there, remember?"

Did she ever. "Finn, you have many fine qualities, but I wouldn't list 'keen powers of observation' among them."

"I'd argue I was watching you pretty closely."

She ignored the double meaning to snap, "Yet you didn't seem to notice when I was imploding personally and professionally."

"Do you actually believe your own press? If I'd thought for a second that you really had half the problems the tabloids accused you of I'd have said something."

"Beyond 'Have another drink, Cait'? You were part of my problem."

"So that's the grounds for your grudge."

"I wouldn't call it a grudge. It's just a memory of that hard-learned lesson."

"Which was…?"

She sighed. "Forget it, Finn."

"No, you're the one who brought it up. If it's the root cause of your attitude, let's clear the air."

She looked around. "I don't think now is the time or place."

"Seems like a good time to me. That way we can move on."

Wasn't that exactly what she wanted? To move on?

"Fine. The truth of the matter is that you were my drug of choice, and like any addict I lived for it and the way it made me feel." The words started out difficult to say, but then the gates opened and everything began to rush out in a flood. "And, just like any other drug, it was destructive. The more I loved you and the more fun we had, the more my world shrank to where you were the only thing. As long as I was on that Finn high I didn't have to worry about living up to my parents' or the public's expectations. I thought I could win the world over by just being me and living my life the way I wanted." She stopped for a breath, and an oddly cathartic feeling washed over her at finally saying it all out loud.

"And what's wrong with that?"

"It might have worked for you, but me… I lost the respect

of my peers, my family, my fans. And the worse it got, the more I let you convince me more of the same was the answer."

Those green eyes met hers in surprise. "I thought we were having a good time."

It was her turn to sigh. "And that's what's so dangerous. And sad. A good time was all you cared about, and I was your good-time girl back then. When it all landed on my head and the press decided I was flaming out, *your* answer was to go to Baja for the weekend."

"I thought you might need to get away for a few days."

"What I *needed* was you to realize that I was in trouble. For you to do something other than shrug it all off. Maybe for you to realize that a drunken Mexican adventure wasn't quite the right way to convince folks that I wasn't one step from rehab."

"That explains what you were ranting about that night."

"And it didn't seem to faze you at all. I'd just lost a really nice endorsement deal because I wasn't considered stable or professional enough, and you didn't care."

"I didn't *know*. There's a difference."

Her temper was burning hot now. So much for not letting him rile her. As much as she hadn't wanted to go there, now she couldn't stop. "Not when the reason you didn't know was because you didn't care enough to actually ask."

"So that's your grudge. I wasn't exactly what you wanted at that exact moment in time. The world can't always revolve around you, you know."

"But it's got to revolve around something." She crossed her arms over her chest. "You've perfected the art of not giving a damn. Somehow it seems to be working for you, but damned if I know how. So there's the root of my so-called grudge. I needed an adult, a partner—not another addict who needed me to enable his quest of thumbing his nose at the whole world."

"Oh, so everything was all *my* fault?"

"I'll take responsibility for my own stupid actions, and I've now paid the price for them."

"To paraphrase my sister-in-law, our mistakes are what make us the people we are today. You seem to be doing all right."

"As do you. And that's what's dangerous for anyone who falls into your orbit. I don't deny that I learned a lot and had a hell of a good time while the times were good. But that doesn't mean that I'm not allowed to have regrets, either."

Finn seemed oddly pleased. "I'm glad you finally admitted it."

"What? That I have regrets?"

"No, that we had a good time."

"There's more to life than a good time."

"That's what life is for."

"You know, Finn, it must be nice to have the world on a platter and no worries at all. But the rest of us aren't that lucky. And that's probably a good thing. One Finn Marshall is more than enough for this world."

"I'm glad I'm unique."

Only Finn could smile in such a way as to make a statement like that sound charming instead of completely worthy of smacking him. Oddly, it took the heat out of her anger. They were never going to fight this out to a solution, but at least she'd said it all.

She laughed quietly. "You know, in a way, so am I."

"What does that mean?"

"Honestly… I don't really know." There weren't words to describe it. "I like you, Finn. Even after all we've been through, you're just impossible *not* to like. I'm not sure I like me, though, when I'm with you. So it's a conundrum. And one that I think is best served by us staying away from each other." She swept the crumbs from her sandwich off the table and stood.

"Hey, Cait?"

She turned.

"You want to know what I remember about that trip to Baja?"

There was a deep purr in his voice that sent shivers over her skin in defiance of the heat, and the light in his eyes made her heart stutter. She swallowed hard. Thinking about Baja made her chest hurt. It encapsulated their entire relationship. For three days she'd been lost in Finn, not knowing that her life was in flames back home—and not caring to check, either. She'd decided she was in love, but that feeling had crashed into reality and she still remembered the gut-punch waiting for her. They'd rehashed enough of their past to know there would be no catharsis waiting on the other side of this topic.

"Not really."

The look on Finn's face called her a liar without him having to say a word. "The Cait that ran off to Baja on a moment's notice wasn't living her life looking over her shoulder or muttering disapprovingly. She wanted to see and do and experience it all. And she wasn't afraid of anything. That Cait was incredible. Do you ever miss her?"

That cut close to the bone, and, damn it, she had the distinct feeling he knew it, too, and had done it on purpose. She felt like a fraud, as if she'd been lying to herself with her new attitude and Finn had stripped it away to uncover the truth under it. Not only had he proved he *did* still know her with that one statement, but she was surprised to find out the urge was still very much there, if buried slightly under the ash of old burns.

Perception shapes reality. She just had to make sure her perceptions didn't backslide and ruin the reality she was creating for herself now.

She took a deep breath. "Finn, as delightful as these little trips down memory lane are, they're really not...pertinent to the here and now. And I'd like to stay focused on *now* and move forward from *here*."

"Then quit worrying so much about the past. Let it go. It doesn't matter now."

"Easy for you to say. I envy that ability of yours sometimes, but I actually care about things beyond my next good time."

"And you think I don't?"

"I know you don't."

There was that look again. The one she couldn't decipher logically enough to judge his reaction to her words. She felt a little bad; her words had been harsh. But how dare he try to downplay everything and forget it with one of his famous and annoying shrugs?

The silence spun out and Caitlyn couldn't figure out what she should—or could—say next. Retreat seemed the safest— if cowardly—option. "I'm going to Makeup now. Bye."

Behind her back, she thought she might have heard Finn laugh quietly.

CHAPTER SIX

CAIT'S ponytail swished against her back as she walked away. He shouldn't spar with her. She was right: it was unprofessional, and not only unnecessary to their working relationship but probably harmful as well. He should just stay the hell away from her, but for reasons he couldn't even begin to understand he couldn't. She'd ignored him for days—which had only nagged at his need to call her on it—but this wasn't exactly where he'd thought they'd end up when he had opened the discussion.

Their conversation had cleared up a lot, but it had raised far more issues, and Cait was insane if she thought she could dump all that out there and then just walk off. He'd been unjustly tried and convicted, and for the first time ever that bothered him.

Plus, he was reeling from the way Cait had almost casually mentioned that she'd been in love with him back then. He doubted she really realized what she'd said, but it had slammed into him with unexpected force. It forced him reevaluate a few things.

They had unfinished business. She might want to pretend that fact didn't exist, but he wasn't playing that game. He was self-aware enough to know she'd dented his ego three years ago, and that might be fueling it some, but he was honest enough to admit that being around her had lit a fire that just couldn't be ignored.

That in itself was unusual, as he'd never had any desire to go back to a woman once things were over. Why did Cait alone have that effect on him? Cait had called him a drug, and at the moment he felt a bit like an addict who'd been given a reminder of what he'd given up and now the craving was consuming him.

And, like a junkie, he was not going to be able to resist.

That was why she was avoiding him—that much was clear now. She, too, was fighting that pull instead of just letting it play out the way it should.

Cait might try to talk a good game, but he'd seen the look on her face when he'd mentioned Baja. She'd given herself a part to play—Caitlyn Reese, Serious Actress and Reformed Sinner—but underneath… Oh, it was still there. She'd just let the pressure and the shame try to force her to be something else. He understood the reaction, but Cait was taking it to new extremes.

And he was just ornery enough to force her to break character and face that fact. It would make things easier in the long run if they got past all of this. She wasn't going to like it, though.

Speaking of things Cait wasn't going to like… He looked at his watch. He needed to be in Wardrobe in ten minutes. Cait was in for one hell of a surprise, and he didn't want to miss a second of it.

An hour later, he wasn't sure he'd made the right choice. Oh, he was forcing her to face facts, but it wasn't going as expected.

"You've got to be kidding me." Cait shot the assistant director a look so dripping with venom that Chris actually backed up a step.

"Caitlyn, honey, what's the problem?"

Finn adjusted the tie of his Army uniform and grinned. "Yeah, Cait, what *is* the problem? I've got a SAG card, so I can both act and produce. It's all legit."

She barely acknowledged he'd spoken, and he could see her fighting to find words that wouldn't come across as ridiculous.

She addressed her question to Chris only. "When did this become amateur hour?"

Chris pulled Cait aside, but Finn could still hear their conversation clearly.

"It's a bit part, and Finn's done this before. I promise you won't have to carry him. He'll make you look good."

Chris thought this was a professional objection, but Finn knew it was personal. He could tell she was torn between acting like a diva or just sucking it up.

"You're trying to tell me there's no one else to do this?"

"This isn't L.A., or even New York. We don't exactly have a wide variety of actors just roaming through the woods in the hopes they'll come across a film set."

"Fine."

Cait adjusted the belt on a dress that made her waist look impossibly tiny. She took a deep breath that nearly caused her breasts to pop the buttons off her blouse. These WWII-era fashions were definitely growing on him. Well, the female fashions, at least. Cait looked fantastic, but his uniform was a bit over-starched. "Let's just do this," she groused. "It's been a very long day already."

As she walked away, Chris turned to him. "Caitlyn's usually so easy to work with. She just must be tired or something. I doubt it's personal…" Chris seemed to catch himself as he put two and two together. "Although maybe it is."

"Oh, I'm sure of it." He grabbed his hat and moved to his place.

He and Cait were pretty much live scenery for most of this scene. One of many couples dancing and chatting in the background while Jason and Naomi had their big emotional thing in the foreground.

Cait took her place across from him at one of the small tables in the pavilion. It was set up festively, like an outdoor party, with candles on the tables and paper lanterns hanging from the exposed beams. A swing band was set up on the other side of a dance floor, and extras milled about.

She kept her voice low. "What? You think you're Alfred Hitchcock now? Making little cameos in your movies?"

"Hitchcock was a director."

"I know that," she snapped. "It makes it even more egocentric to cast yourself in a movie when you're just the producer."

"*Just* the producer? What happened to how hard-working and professional I am?"

Cait bit her lip. He assumed she hadn't realized he'd seen her little interview already.

"That was before I knew you were vain enough to do this."

"It's not vanity. This is a present for my grandfather."

"You couldn't get him a tie or something?"

"The man has everything already. Except a movie."

After a brief frown, Cait ignored him while they did the light check, but she definitely wasn't happy. Maybe he shouldn't have pushed this. If her anger was going to affect her performance...

He shouldn't have worried. When Cait opened her eyes the anger was gone, proving once again she was a pro. As the cues came, she leaned in and propped her chin on her fist. A small flirtatious smile played over her lips and his body hardened. *She's only acting.* But, damn, she was good.

"We're supposed to be talking and flirting, remember? I thought you'd decided you were an actor now."

Her voice was barely above a whisper—just enough for

him to hear without creating additional noise on the set—but the challenge was there in her words and in her eyes.

He could never resist a challenge.

He leaned forward as well, letting his eyes rake over her. "I don't even have to act. I've been wanting to tell you for days how beautiful you are. I didn't think you could get more beautiful, but you did."

Cait's eyes widened and her lips parted in shock.

"It's so hard not to kiss you and see if you taste as good as you look. If it's as good as I remember." Taking hold of her hand, he let his thumb trace over the soft skin of her wrist. "Your skin…it was always so soft, so smooth under my hands, my tongue. And you loved being touched almost as much as I loved touching you." He felt her pulse jump, and her tongue rubbed over her bottom lip.

He was growing hard, uncomfortably so, and Cait was in real danger if she didn't stop looking at him like that. Her smile was frozen in place, but the heat in her eyes scorched him. This had turned into something far more dangerous than he'd predicted.

He pulled himself together forcefully. Leaning a little bit closer, he whispered, "How's that for acting?"

Cait's façade slipped the tiniest bit, but only someone paying close attention would have noticed. She swallowed hard, and the heat in her gaze faded to something else. She slid her wrist out of his hand and traced her finger over the rim of her glass instead. "Pretty average, actually."

He'd give her credit for a quick recovery—especially since he was having such a hard time doing the same. "You're a hard woman, Cait."

"And you're a—"

"Cut!"

Cait smirked, but kept silent as the crew quickly reset for a second take. When the cue came, Cait leaned in again. "You're supposed to be flirting with me, not trying to seduce me."

"There's a difference?"

"Of course. Flirting is a game. It's about the thrill of the chase. Seduction focuses solely on results."

Her scolding words were at odds with the flirtatious look on her face. It bordered on confusing. Although he knew she was playing to the cameras, there was something genuine as well. Like the smile she'd worn the other night... He remembered the reality too well to believe it was *all* an act.

"You don't play games, Cait. It's not in your nature. You look for the genuine. That's part of your charm."

She batted her eyelashes and gave him a sly smile. "I have charm?"

"Oh, definitely. That's why I'm trying to seduce you."

She faltered before she cut her eyes at him. "But I'm Rebecca right now, not Caitlyn. And you're not the hero of this story, so you don't get to seduce the girl."

The pressure against his zipper bordered on painful now, and Finn silently admitted the full truth he'd been denying. He wanted her. Badly. Their attraction had always been intensely physical, and his body was remembering that with a vengeance. It was only his big brain that continued to fight it. Coupled with the way Cait kept eyeballing him like a tasty treat... She was damn lucky there were two dozen people standing around and the cameras were rolling.

Of course maybe that was why she thought she could get away with it. She wanted the game? The thrill of the chase? Fine.

Game on, Cait.

Tugging at the collar of his uniform, he reminded her, "But I'm going off to war. I may never know the love of a woman again. You'd deny me one last touch? A taste? A sweet memory to take to battle with me?"

She swallowed hard. "Been there, done that."

He let his eyes roam over her again until she started to blush. "Yeah, I remember."

"Well, then, you don't need—"

"My question is…" He waited until her eyes met his again. "Do you?"

Cait looked away, but not before he saw her unguarded reaction. *She did.* That much was clear. And, for all her prim talk, the memory was a good one. *Oh, Caity,* he thought, *you forgot that I always play to win.*

Damn Finn. What the hell kind of game was he playing? "Torture Caitlyn" seemed an obvious answer, and he was doing a damn fine job of it.

Finn seemed to be waiting, and Caitlyn scrambled to find the proper words—or even the proper tone.

Because she remembered, all right. Hell, she couldn't seem to remember anything else these days.

"Well…" she hedged, only to be saved, once again, by the wonderful sound of the word, "Cut!"

Finn grinned, seemingly aware of her relief that she didn't have to answer right now.

Caitlyn looked away, unable to keep eye contact, only to meet Naomi's killing glare. So Naomi was feeling a little possessive of Finn? That possessiveness didn't sit well with Caitlyn, but she refused to examine it. Their next scene together was going to be fun. Naomi wouldn't have to dig too deep to find her motivation. In fact, Caitlyn wouldn't be surprised if Naomi "accidentally" slapped her for real.

With the cameras reset and rolling, she had to turn her attention back to Finn. "Naomi is not happy."

"She never is."

She happened to agree, but to do so aloud would be catty. "Then why do you put up with her?"

"Because I have to be nice to the talent."

"I meant off the set." She stirred the drink in front of her.

"Because I, too, am a team player."

It was hard to keep a smile on her face for the camera with their conversation taking such strange turns, but she was having a hard time separating what parts of the conversations were real and which ones weren't. Finn didn't seem to be having that problem. While he'd given her looks that practically melted her insides, he was doing an admirable job of pasting a camera-perfect smile across his face as well.

"What?"

"What what? She's vain and needy, but I hold up my end of the deal, same as you."

Now she was totally lost. "As me?"

"How do *you* put up with Jason's vanity and neediness—not to mention his stupidity?"

"By limiting exposure."

"Same here."

It was difficult not to react to that statement. "Lord, Finn, I know you've perfected the art of not giving a damn, but that's really…slimy, actually."

He actually looked insulted. He quickly reschooled his face, though. "What do you mean by that?"

"Naomi's not my favorite person, but it's unfair to use her like that. She seems to care for you, and it's wrong for you to lead her on like that when you don't care for her." *And I would know.*

He had the nerve to laugh at her. "You think I'm sleeping with Naomi?"

"Aren't you?"

"God, no. My 'relationship' with Naomi is no different than your relationship with Jason."

Why did that make a little happy bubble inflate in her chest? "Then I owe you an apology. But I still have to say that I don't think she knows that. In fact, if looks could kill I'd be dead on the floor right now."

There was that shrug again. "Oh, she knows it. It's just her irrational jealousy of you in general that's drawing the killing looks."

She'd adjusted—well, almost—to the idea of Finn and Naomi, so the paradigm shift took a minute to process. She didn't realize Walter had called "cut" until the camera moved closer to her and Finn to get close-ups and cutaways. The pensive looks were easy to do; Lord knew she had enough on her mind to ponder. The smiley and giggly ones were a bit harder, and when they asked Finn to take her hand again for some close-ups her insides got wobbly. Eventually Walter was satisfied, and she sent up a sigh of thanks.

Caitlyn had never felt so off-kilter during a shoot before. Between the death stares from Naomi, the sly smiles from Finn and the confused looks of the crew when she was a second too slow picking up on instructions... *Ugh.* She needed to get a hold of herself. Quickly. The sooner this scene was over, the better. She closed her eyes and searched for her center.

When she was called to her next mark, what little focus she'd found seemed to slither away. She'd rehearsed this scene with an extra, and normally it would be a piece of cake. They were supposed to dance—well, sway, at least—until Jason's character got jealous enough to pull her away. A hysterical laugh caught in her throat. It was almost ridiculous, considering their past, the fiasco in D.C. that night, and the current supposed love-tangle between Finn, Jason, Naomi and her.

She paced slowly, focusing on Rebecca until it was time. She just hoped she'd found *enough* focus as she took a deep breath to steel herself to do one thing she'd never thought she'd do again: wrap her arms around Finn and let him hold her.

And it nearly took her breath away.

She'd forgotten how solid he was. How much heat he generated. But what she hadn't forgotten was the feel of him, the right place to align herself to curl perfectly against his chest, the position her head needed to be in so that Finn's cheek could rest against her forehead. When Finn's fingers twined through hers to pull their hands against his chest, her knees wobbled from the onslaught of sensation and memory.

"You okay?" His voice came from above her head, but she could hear it through the ear pressed against his chest as well.

"Just lost my balance there for a second. It's these shoes," she added.

"Of course." But Finn laughed as he said it, and it rumbled under her cheek.

Dear heaven, the man was made to wear a uniform. She'd never known she could be such a sucker for a man in uniform, but then she'd never seen one—felt one, actually—filled out quite so nicely, either. Someone called "Action!" and as everyone came to life around them, she and Finn swayed to imaginary music.

No matter how many times she tried to remind herself that it was all just for show, Finn's earlier words were still too fresh in her mind. The slow, seductive movements were melting her insides, causing her to feel languid and liquid.

"This feels familiar," he mumbled.

"Indeed." It was all she could manage at the moment. Her throat was too tight and her insides were too jumbled. She closed her eyes and inhaled deeply, letting the scent of him fill her lungs. Memories and emotions swirled through her. This was not good. It felt good—better than good—but deep down she knew it shouldn't and wasn't.

A small ache settled in her chest. She didn't want to name it, because that would only make it worse. She bit the inside of her lip and let the pain bring her back to reality.

Or whatever the hell she could call *this* situation. If anything, it had crossed the line into surreal. The layers of ridiculousness meshed and the lines blurred. She was flirting with her real-life ex who was pretending to be her potential new love on camera, while her pretend new on-camera love, whom she didn't even like in real life, got jealous of the actions of the woman she was pretending to be. All while her ex-friend, who was pretending to be her sister, seethed with pretend jealousy over the pretend new love, while honestly seething with jealousy over her ex, who was pretending... *Ugh.* It made her head hurt when she tried to untangle it.

"It makes it easier, though."

She tilted her head up to look at Finn. Nothing about this was easy. "What does?"

Those green eyes sucked her in and held her. "The fact we've done this before. What do you call it? Method?"

She swallowed, unable to break away from those eyes. "Yeah. It's supposed to give a more genuine performance."

"It's too bad, then, that I'm not supposed to be seducing you. I could give a very genuine performance of that right now."

She could feel the proof of that statement pressing against her, and it sent a shiver over her skin as a fire sparked to life in her belly. *Oh, so could I.*

Thankfully, she heard the cue and was prepared for the hand that clasped around her elbow and jerked. Finn stiffened, but released her, and the two men glowered at each other. Then Jason was dragging her through the crowd out of the frame.

It was easy enough to act bewildered and clumsy. And, though the script didn't call for it, she couldn't help but look over her shoulder.

Finn didn't look happy. And that look was real. It shook

her insides, making her realize how dangerous this actually was.

And she still had at least one more take to do.

It was late. It had been a very long day. He was tired. Cait was most likely exhausted. If he had a lick of sense he'd be headed back to his place for a cold shower and a good night's sleep.

But, as his brothers were constantly telling him, he was an idiot. And, Finn thought, there was a chance he was about to really prove them right this time. There was no way he could *not* do this.

He parked his motorcycle a block from Cait's rented condo and walked the rest of the way, keeping to the shadows outside the streetlights' glow. While Cait hadn't mentioned any problems with the paparazzi staking out her place, that didn't mean he was totally in the clear. The last thing he wanted right now was a run-in with the press. Several others of the cast and crew were staying either in this complex or nearby, so if he was seen, the dots didn't *have* to connect to Cait. Not that a camera would put him off his mission, but he hoped he wouldn't have to deal with that. He simply didn't have the patience at the moment.

His official capacity meant he had access to the rental agreement, which included the code for the gate. He felt no guilt or hesitation at using it instead of calling up and hoping Cait would let him in. Once inside the walled courtyard, he let out at small sigh of relief he'd gotten in unobserved and took the steps up to her door two at a time.

He'd left the set only a few minutes after she had, so she couldn't have been home very long. He could see lights on inside. Finn rang the bell and waited.

He could hear movement, but the lag between the noise and the sound of the lock being flipped could only mean Cait wasn't thrilled to see him on her doorstep and had debated before deciding to open the door.

But she did open it, albeit only a foot or so. Her body blocked the opening. "It's really late, Finn," she said in lieu of a greeting.

"I know."

"And I'm tired."

"I figured."

Cait's teeth caught her bottom lip. For someone who claimed to be tired—and should be tired—she looked remarkably alert. She'd removed all the makeup from earlier, allowing her own natural beauty to glow with that girl-next-door goodness. And without all the mascara her eyes seemed brighter.

While she'd brushed the old-fashioned style out, her hair still held a bit of the curl, giving her reddish-gold waves around her face. She wore an overlarge tee shirt with the London Underground symbol on it. He could see the hard peaks of her nipples, and his hands itched to trace them. The shirt swallowed her almost to the hem of her frayed cutoffs. Those long, shapely legs were bare.

Cait shifted her weight, balancing one bare foot on top of the other, and leaned against the doorframe. "So what brings you by?"

He caught her stare and held it. "I think you know."

There was no surprise or shock, not even a trace of outrage at his statement. Her face remained still; the only indication she'd heard him was a slight hitch in her breathing. "What makes you think I'd let you in?"

"Because you want to."

She shook her head and snorted. "God, you're cocky."

He stepped closer and Cait had to lift her chin to keep eye contact. There was annoyance in those eyes, but that wasn't all that was simmering there. It had the same effect on him as a caress. "No, just honest. I've never lied to you, never taken you anywhere you didn't want to go. If I'm wrong—" and he knew now he wasn't "—just say so and I'll leave."

He knew that look on her face. She was arguing with herself, trying to talk herself into a different position. It annoyed him. He'd taken the bigger step, showing up here. She had to cross the remaining distance.

Cait dithered so long Finn began to wonder if he'd read the situation wrong, after all.

Then, in a flash, Cait's mouth landed on his.

He froze. Although this was what he'd come for—the logical outcome of the simmering tension of the last few days— the reality of Cait's lips pressed against his still came as a shock to his body.

Just as quickly, though, the paralysis broke and he grabbed for her face, holding her steady as her mouth opened under his and his tongue slipped inside.

Cait jumped as if she'd touched a live wire and her hands clasped around his biceps in a vise-like grip. It was easy, then, to walk back a step or two and move them both inside the door.

She responded by boosting herself up, wrapping her legs around his waist and using one foot to push the door closed with a bang.

Anchored against him now, Cait let her kiss turn carnal, and he could taste the desire that drove her.

It set him on fire.

This was what he'd tried to forget, what he'd let himself pretend he *could* forget: the sharp-clawed need that Cait brought roaring to life inside him. It blotted out everything that wasn't Cait, shrinking the universe to the woman who felt like a flame in his arms.

They weren't going to make it to the bedroom. Hell, he wasn't going to make it to the couch. Her touch robbed him of all control, went deep inside him to shine light on all his secrets and made him feel invincible at the same time. He sank to his knees, then let Cait push him back onto the carpet. She covered him like an erotic blanket, her legs tangling around his until she captured his thigh and rocked against it with a groan.

The sensation of Finn's thigh pressing against her core sent a shock wave through Cait that blurred the edges of her vision. She was already on the edge; the last few days had primed her for this moment, and it wouldn't take much effort on Finn's part to take her the rest of the way.

She could feel a similar urgency in him; the skin under her hands thrummed with energy and restrained desire, and it only fed the flames licking at her. But she also knew Finn—her body certainly did—and she knew that urgency would not translate to speed. Finn might be hungry, but he wouldn't be rushed. The thought sent an anticipatory shiver through her.

Rising to her knees, she grabbed the hem of her shirt and pulled it over her head. Finn's hands had been at her hips, holding her, but they now slid up over her waist and ribs until he cupped her breasts, his thumbs rasping over her nipples until she nearly sobbed at the sensation.

She needed to touch him, too. To feel his skin under her hands again. She tugged his shirt out of the waist of his jeans and pushed it up. *Mercy.* Finn hadn't let himself go in the intervening years. If anything, the ridges defining his torso were more pronounced. She felt a bit embarrassed over the few pounds she'd gained. But then Finn pushed himself up to peel the shirt the rest of the way off and pulled her back to the floor with him, giving her skin-to-skin contact that nearly scorched her.

She ran her tongue along his neck, and the familiar taste of his skin brought back memories of other times, other places.

The growl that came from deep in his throat only sharpened the clarity of what she was doing.

It was insane. It was stupid.

It was inevitable.

From the moment she'd learned Finn was heading this project she'd known, deep down, that this would happen. Even more disturbing was the fact she'd rather *hoped* it would happen.

Pressing her to her back, Finn captured a nipple in his mouth, and there was no room for anything anymore. Only pleasure. Pleasure that nearly overwhelmed her.

It didn't mean anything, she told herself almost desperately. She could enjoy it for what it was and nothing more.

It was hard to think, but she really didn't want to, either. Nothing really made sense, anyway. Except this.

This was what got you in trouble last time. It was a sobering thought, but not one that could hold up against the moist heat of Finn's mouth as he revisited all the places he knew would drive her wild. That place on her neck. The back of her knee. Everything became a sensual blur, and she bit her lip to keep from screaming. She might pay for this in the morning, but sometimes the high was well worth the hangover.

Then his head dipped between her thighs, and the touch of his tongue drove her right over the edge.

She recovered enough to open her eyes and focus in time to see Finn kneeling between her legs as he rolled on a condom. His eyes were dark as he met hers, and she knew he was getting close himself.

But his smile was a wicked promise as trailed his fingers along her inner thigh. "You still with me, Caity?"

In answer, she wrapped a hand around his hard length. A hiss escaped through his clenched jaw, and his fingers dug into her hips as she guided him into position.

Was that groan his? Or hers? It all blurred together as Finn slid in with agonizing, deliberate slowness until their hips met and he buried his face in her shoulder.

Cait could feel his heart slamming against his chest, and a poignant pang cut through the haze as Finn twined his fingers through hers and sighed deeply. The connection was complete. Electric. Perfect.

And terrifying. It stirred up too much inside her to not scare her.

Then Finn pushed up to his elbows and began to move.

And nothing mattered after that.

CHAPTER SEVEN

"You're going to kill me, Caity." Finn spoke to the top of Cait's head. She was sprawled across his chest, breathing heavily, but he felt her laugh. She rolled off to the side, arms spread wide over the bed as she gasped for air.

"Not if you kill me first." She stretched and smiled. "But I'll die a happy woman, that's for sure."

They'd made it to the bedroom after the second—third?—time. He'd lost count, trapped as he was in Cait's erotic web. He should be sated, exhausted, but he didn't seem to have Cait out of his system yet, and the need to touch her hadn't abated. Desire still curled through him, as if he had to make up for lost time.

Cait sat up and reached for her water on the bedside table. As she did, he noticed a scar above her right elbow. It looked recently acquired, but thoroughly healed. He ran his fingers over it. "I don't remember seeing this on the set."

"Makeup does a really good job covering it." She stiffened, then twisted and tried to see over her shoulder. "Oh, hell, do I have carpet burns? I still have one more scene in a swim-suit tomorrow, and I'll never be able to explain those away."

"No carpet burns." She let out a sigh of relief that caused him to laugh and earned him a half-hearted swat. "But where'd you get this?"

"Remember that night on Sunset with the guy and the camera?"

Of course. They'd been coming out of a club—pretty trashed, granted—but it had been the paparazzo that jumped in front of them, camera flashing, that had caused Cait to miss the curb and fall. She'd landed wrong and banged her arm up pretty bad. The pictures of her flat on her back had made the papers—as had the ones of him swinging for the cameraman. He'd nearly been arrested and the media circus had been a nightmare. But... "Where did the scar come from, though?"

"It turned out I actually broke the bone, and since it was never set it didn't heal properly. It kept bothering me, until I finally went and had it checked last year. They had to go in and re-break it and put in a pin. The doc says the scar will fade eventually." She grinned and snuggled back against his side. "Remember that one blogger who kept calling us self-destructive? Well, I now have the scar that might prove he was on to something. Looking back, I'm surprised I don't have a lot more scars to show."

She was laughing, but he didn't find it funny. She'd talked about lasting damage, but he'd never thought it would be literal and physical. Guilt nagged at him. It was a new feeling that sat awkwardly on his shoulders, and he didn't like it. "I didn't know you'd hurt yourself that bad."

"I know that, Finn." She pushed up onto her elbow and the smile was gone. "And I'm not blaming you for it. Accidents happen. It's not like we were poster children for personal responsibility. We're just lucky that was the worst of it."

"Yet you still carry a grudge for everything else?"

She grinned. "Absolutely. I'll accept my fair share of responsibility, but I reserve the right to be grudgey."

He ran a hand down her back and over her butt. "And this makes sense how, then?"

"It doesn't. But, then, I've never associated Finn Marshall

with good decision-making, anyway. That's probably part of what makes you so hard for me to resist."

He understood the feeling, and as the silence stretched out that feeling warmed him. Then she sighed and pushed the rest of the way up to a seated position.

"And on that note, it's probably time for you to be leaving."

The words hit him like cold water. "What?"

"We both have to work tomorrow. I need to sleep for a couple of hours—and you do, too. But in a couple of hours the neighborhood will be waking up, and I really don't want anyone to see you leaving here."

He'd had similar thoughts, but rationality had a hard time holding up against the feel of Cait's skin against his. "You're kidding me." When she shook her head, irritation slid over him. "Ashamed of yourself, are you?"

"Just don't feel like dealing with the fallout. There's enough melodrama out there already without making this a real soap opera."

Technically, Cait had dodged the question, but he didn't call her on it. She rolled off the bed and to her feet. She found a tee shirt on the floor and pulled it over her head before disappearing out into the hallway. A minute later she returned, carrying his clothes, and dropped them on the bed.

It seemed she was serious. "You're kicking me out?"

"Not exactly." She smiled, but it was weak and slightly humorless. "Just encouraging you to leave without feeling any guilt for not staying the night."

"I suddenly feel cheap and tawdry."

She cut her eyes at him. "You're the one who showed up on my porch looking for a booty call."

"That's not…" He trailed off as Cait lifted an eyebrow at him in disbelief. "*Entirely* true."

"There was *another* reason bringing you to my door in the middle of the night?"

Damn it. He'd trade his trust fund for a good answer—if for no other reason than to remove that look from her face. He reached for his shirt instead, and heard her snort as he pulled it on.

Cait got ready for bed as he got dressed, and while she didn't exactly shove him out the door there wasn't much in the way of a proper goodbye. She had the lights off before he was even fully down the stairs.

It did feel rather tawdry—regardless of her valid reason for kicking him out.

And he didn't like it at all.

It was another hot, sticky day on the set and everyone's tempers were running on short fuses. Except Caitlyn's.

She was exhausted and distracted, but the endorphins still flowing through her body kept her temper at bay. She had too much on her mind, anyway, to get pulled into petty squabbles, and, since she really didn't want to accidentally say something she might regret later, she claimed a headache. Asking one of the production assistants to come get her when they were ready for her, she went back to her trailer to lie down.

The sleep she'd supposedly kicked Finn out in order to get hadn't come for a long while. She'd known what would happen if she let Finn in last night, but there hadn't been a way to resist the irresistible.

Was it smart? No. But then hadn't she decided their entire relationship showed a remarkable lack of good judgment? She allowed herself a tiny smile. Finn would be hard to resist even if she didn't have so many memories of how good they could be together—physically, at least. Had it been enjoyable? Oh, definitely.

But that didn't stop her from regretting it. Just a little. Sex only confused things, complicating an already complicated situation. Just when she felt she'd figured out who she wanted to be, Finn threw three years of soul-searching and planning out the window with a smile and a kiss. And that meant she hadn't really changed that much at all.

Her excuse for making him leave last night had been valid, but it had also been a much-needed out from the situation. Something had awakened inside her and she needed time to sort out what that meant. She was just glad he hadn't flat-out asked to stay, because she would have had a very hard time saying no.

And she probably would have slept much better with Finn as her pillow, because Finn made everything seem so easy. Accept something at face value for what it was and it became simple. Addictive.

She was smart enough to know that not all things that felt good—or even slightly right—were necessarily good in the long run. But even that knowledge didn't allow her to relax, and the minutes ticked by slowly as she stared at the ceiling.

"Fifteen minutes, Caitlyn." The knock on her door and the voice brought her back to earth.

She gave herself a strong shake. It probably had been inevitable, but she had it out of her system now. People went back to their exes all the time for a little relief, so she could cut herself some slack, chalk it up to the shock of being around Finn again and go back to her original plan.

Feeling resolved and more focused, Caitlyn grabbed her water bottle and went back to the set.

That resolve lasted all of five minutes, as Finn was deep in conversation with the assistant director not five feet from where she needed to be. She looked inward for focus and shrugged out of her robe. She made the mistake of looking at Finn as she draped it over the back of her chair.

His smile was appreciative, not leering, but it still had

her tugging at the bodice of the bathing suit. But there was a warmth in his eyes, too, that knocked her off balance a little.

Even more disturbing was the little glow that it lit inside her chest.

Ah, hell.

Finn felt a bit foolish watching Cait's trailer from the window of the office trailer. It was late, and everything shut down for the day hours ago, yet Cait hadn't returned to her trailer. Her rental car was still there, meaning she hadn't returned to the city for the night, but he didn't know where she was. Her trailer was dark, but there were lights on in some of the others, indicating she was in one of them. But short of going door-to-door looking for her...

No, he might feel foolish, but there was no reason to act foolish as well.

He glanced back to the email that was half-occupying his attention, and when he looked up, he saw the door to Cait's trailer close and the light inside come on. He shut down the computer and crossed the short distance separating the trailers.

He didn't bother to knock, and Cait merely looked up in surprise. "Oh, it's you. What's up?"

Her beautiful hair was pulled up in a ponytail that curled over her shoulder before she tossed it back in an impatient gesture. In a pair of frayed and tattered jeans, a tee shirt that hugged her curves and flip-flops, she looked like a fresh-faced college student. The battered leather backpack he remembered only completed the look, but that didn't stop the lust that had been kept simmering all day from roiling to a boil in his veins.

He wanted to pounce on her at the same time as he simply wanted to enjoy the moment and prolong it. "You're here late tonight."

"As are you," she said, then rubbed her hands over her face like she was frustrated. "There is a cold beer and a hot bath calling my name, so…"

He ignored the hint. "Why so stressed?"

"Not stressed. Just tired. I've spent the last two hours reading through with Naomi and Jason for tomorrow. It's exhausting."

He sat on the little couch. "Something not right?"

She dropped her backpack and sat at the other end, scrubbing a hand across her face. "Oh… No… I mean, it's fine. Just tense. And the tension is quite draining."

"If Naomi's giving you a hard time…"

She sighed and seemed to sink into the cushions as she leaned back and closed her eyes. "I can handle her. In a way it's funny—sad funny, not ha-ha funny. If I didn't know better, I'd feel bad. But it's her problem, not mine. And it's going to make that scene really amazing." She opened her eyes and smiled tiredly. "And that's what matters, right?"

Finn didn't know if he should feel insulted or not at her casual attitude. After all but kicking him out last night, she'd pretty much avoided him all day today. And while he'd caught at least one look thrown in his direction that defied interpretation, she was otherwise acting as if nothing at all had happened.

And these days he had no idea what was acting and what wasn't.

But something had happened. *That* had been real, and it called him back to her tonight against all good sense.

"Is this going to take long?" She pushed to her feet and went to stand front of her fridge with the door open and a pensive look on her face.

Her words collided hard with thoughts headed in a direction of what would take all night. He shook himself. "What?"

"Whatever you're here for."

What *was* he here for, exactly? Oh, he knew what his body wanted, but for the first time ever he felt oddly conflicted. This was new and disturbing—and it was a feeling he associated only with Cait. "It might. Why?"

"Then I'm going to open this." She held up a beer bottle. A bump of her hip had the door closed and she was screwing the top off. "I don't normally drink at all on the set, but I do keep one on hand in case of an emergency. Want half? I'll fall asleep on the way home if I drink the whole thing."

"Lightweight," he teased, but he nodded as well.

"I swore off alcohol for a while when I moved to London. All those people who were 'concerned about my drinking problem—'" she included the air quotes "—should be glad to hear I haven't had more than a buzz in three years."

"So the rumors about rehab…"

Cait poured half the beer in a coffee cup before offering him the bottle and keeping the cup for herself. Instead of returning to the couch to sit, she leaned against the table. "Aren't true. Once I got away from everything—my parents, the press…" She trailed off and wouldn't meet his eyes.

"Me?"

She looked up, considering, before she finally nodded. "Yes, even you to a degree. My stress levels went way down and I had less need to find solace in a bottle. I found healthier ways to deal with things—meditation, yoga…" At his laugh, she stopped. "What?"

"A California girl has to move to London to discover meditation and yoga? That's got to be a first."

That finally earned him a smile. "I even became a vegetarian for a while, but bacon tempted me back. I love British bacon. I think I gained ten pounds from bacon alone."

"It looks good on you." He let his eyes wander over her until she began to blush. "I'm serious. You used to take starving starlet to a new level."

"Just another thing I didn't have to worry about once I left." Cait finally moved back to her place on the couch. This time when she sat, she left her shoes on the floor and stretched her legs across the cushions with another deep sigh. "By the way, one of the P.A.s mentioned that your brother and his wife are going to be extras tomorrow?"

He sat the bottle on the table and lifted her feet into his lap. Digging his thumbs into the ball of her foot, he began to rub them the way she liked. She groaned and closed her eyes in pleasure. "Ethan and Lily. They're pretty much just scenery, so don't worry that it will be amateur hour."

She opened one eye. "I guess I should apologize for that crack. You did a great job." He warmed a little, because that wasn't a compliment Cait would throw out casually. "My question, though, is why has this become a family affair?"

"Like I said, *Folly* is a present for my grandfather. Putting his grandchildren in it is just an extra surprise."

"That's really sweet of you." Cait's forehead wrinkled as something occurred to her, then she nodded. "Ah, I understand now."

His hands stilled. "Understand what?"

She wiggled toes painted a garish shade of red until his fingers started to move again. "Why you've been so involved and constantly hovering over this project."

"Because the damn thing is a three-ring circus."

She shook her head as his hands moved to her calf and squeezed the muscle. "No. This is the one thing your brothers can't do for your grandfather."

Her perceptiveness caught him off-guard. He'd never hidden the fact that this film had personal importance to him because of Granddad, but he'd never said anything about his brothers. Cait had always managed to get deeper under his skin than he liked, but still… He frowned at her.

"Oh, don't do that. Probably no one else but me has figured that out. You don't give a damn about much, but your grandparents are the exception. So I understand."

"And what makes you think—?"

"You tend to talk a lot when you're drunk." She grinned at him.

"I do not."

"You do, honey. Or you did, at least. Your family was one of your favorite topics, and I can read between the lines. Your brothers live close to home, do the family business thing and they're the 'good' ones. But, no matter what they do for your grandfather, making him a film is something only *you* can do. I think it's wonderful, and I'm honored to be a part of it." She lifted the coffee cup in a mock toast. "Here's to making your family proud of their wild child."

So she wanted to dig into psyches tonight? Fine. He could play that game. "And yours," he added, lifting the bottle.

She stiffened, but didn't say anything.

"Oh, come on, Cait, you outright babble when you're drunk. You think I don't know that you're out to prove something to your parents? You always were, and I don't see a stint in exile changing that. In fact, some might say it's what's fueling your return."

Her mouth twisted, but she didn't try to deny it. "Then here's to living up to expectations. For once. May we both be successful."

"Those are two different things, Cait."

"Maybe for you," she scoffed. "I think we've established that the rest of us see the world a little differently."

"Maybe *you* established that. I don't agree."

Cait lifted her hands in surrender. "I'm too tired to fight with you again."

He gentled the massage into a caress. "That's certainly not why I'm here."

"I figured that much." She pulled her legs out of his lap

and curled them up to her chest. Wrapping her arms around them, she rested her cheek on her knees. "And it's tempting, but I don't think it's wise."

It took him a second to figure that out, and the rejection stung. It was tempered, however, by the sigh of regret in her voice. "And that's because…?"

"It's not healthy. Or fair, really, for me to use you that. Like a crutch."

He didn't fully understand her words. "I'm a crutch?"

She nodded, but her lips twisted. "Coming home is tough—tougher than I thought—but I shouldn't lean on you to make it easier for me. I think I need to stand on my own this time instead of using you to prop me up. It's wrong."

"I'm not complaining."

"No." She chuckled. "You wouldn't. But if I'm going to get my life back on track, I can't get all tangled up with you again. To be honest, you're dangerously addictive, and I don't see it ending well."

"You're over-thinking this."

"That would be a first for me, wouldn't it? Actually thinking something through before acting?"

"You're too hard on yourself. You always have been. There were expectations on you, but you let them get to you too much. And if you want to be all self-helpy about it, *that* was what nearly destroyed you three years ago. If you want your comeback, make it on your terms. Otherwise you'll end up back where you were before you left."

She snorted. "When did you get such insights into the human psyche?"

"It's not the human psyche. It's *your* psyche. Like I said, I was watching you pretty closely at the time."

Cait was quiet for a moment, but it wasn't an uncomfortable silence, so he let it spin out until she said with a soft smile, "Maybe I was wrong."

"I'll agree to that in general terms, because I like to be right, but for the sake of this conversation maybe you should be more specific."

"When I said that we weren't friends… In a strange way, I'm beginning to see that we were."

"Are," he corrected. Somehow it seemed very important to make that clear.

"Friends with benefits?" she challenged.

"I've never lied to you, Cait, and I won't start now."

"I know. And I think that's probably why you're so dangerous for me. The honesty can be brutal, but it's refreshing all the same, and it does make it easier in the long run." She laughed at her words. "No misunderstandings."

He met her eyes. "It's easier that way."

Cait pushed to her knees, and Finn wondered if he'd missed something. But when she crawled over the few feet separating them on the narrow couch and threw a leg over to straddle his lap, he assumed she'd worked it all out in her head. His hands went to her waist automatically, fitting perfectly into the soft indentation below her ribs and splaying down to the waistband of her jeans.

Her hand cupped his jaw, and the butterfly-light caress of her thumb across his lips sent lightning through his veins. "I still don't think…"

The ends of her ponytail brushed across the tips of his fingers, and he wrapped the silky strands around his fist. The light scent of her perfume tickled his nose. "Then don't think so much. Just take what you want. What you need."

He caught her smile as her head dipped to his.

The craving for her was still there, springing to the fore at the first taste, but it was tempered more than expected. The edge wasn't as sharp, and something else had filled the gap. Something that was quintessentially Cait. His hands shook slightly as they pulled her closer to him, molding her body into his.

Take what you want. Cait didn't know what she wanted— other than this, *now*. Right and wrong were too easily confused when it was Finn leading her down the path. Her skin sizzled to life under his hands, the nerves overly sensitive to his touch. She was fascinated by the play of muscles under tanned skin as he peeled his shirt over his head and removed hers. Those shoulders looked broad enough to support the weight of the world, and once upon a time she'd wanted them to support her. This time, that was exactly what he was offering—however temporarily—and there were no strings attached.

Finn's hands worked the snap of her jeans, releasing the zipper and letting his fingers fill the gap between denim and skin, and his mouth left shivers in its wake as it moved down her neck to the sensitive skin over her collarbone. The muscles in her neck felt weak, and her head tipped back to give him greater access. As his tongue moved to the hollow at the base of her throat, she let her hand slide down his chest to his straining zipper.

She traced the bulge and Finn's groan reverberated through her. She wanted to move closer, press herself against him... Cursing the narrow couch and the difficulties of jeans, Cait slid off Finn's lap.

His eyes were bright as he watched her wiggle both jeans and panties down to step out of them. Arching his hips, he mirrored her movements and his clothes landed on hers on the floor.

Then he settled back onto the couch and extended a hand to her. Taking it, she let Finn reposition her, her thighs framing his, as she lowered herself inch by inch. His hands splayed across her back, holding her against his heat, and the shudder that started in him ended in her.

Cait let her forehead rest on his, and his breath cooled the skin of her neck, leaving goose bumps. She held still, just enjoying the moment and the sensation. Then Finn's hands moved to her hips, and she let the sensations take over completely.

Right or wrong, this was honest. It was what she needed and what she wanted, and she was happy to take what Finn was willing to give.

She'd carried a knot in her stomach for so long, the lack of it felt strange. Strange enough that it took her several hours to identify what was different about her today.

The cynic in her just wanted to chalk it up to several toe-curling orgasms and file it away under "you just needed to get laid." But sex wasn't *that* good a cure-all. Not even sex with Finn.

No, her whole attitude was different today. Even the heat seemed more bearable today as she rested in her chair under a tent between takes. Naomi's little temper tantrums seemed more sad than anything else, and Jason's ego simply amused her. Her co-stars weren't her problem.

So she had to assume it was Finn. Late last night she'd realized that she wasn't just living down her past with the public. She was also living it down to herself, looking for forgiveness for the spectacular way she'd destroyed everything she had. Out of spite and weakness, she'd let her demons drive her almost as if she wanted to bring it all down. And deep down she probably had wanted to. Being around—and with—Finn again had rather brought her full circle, and she was ready to pick up where she'd left off.

Finn seemed to have forgiven her. She was slowly forgiving herself. Everything else had to be earned. She knew what she wanted now, and she could only earn those things the hard way. But she was in a good place to do so. She'd found herself again.

"Ms. Reese?"

Caitlyn shook herself out of her reverie to see a young, dark-haired woman approaching. Based on her clothes, the woman must be one of the extras, but the extras weren't normally allowed to roam free on the set like this. "Yes?" she answered cautiously.

"I just wanted to introduce myself. I'm Lily Marshall."

The name took a minute to penetrate. "Finn's sister-in-law?"

Lily nodded. "That's Ethan—he's mine—over there with Finn."

Caitlyn followed Lily's finger to the man laughing with Finn. For all he liked to complain about his brothers, there was a certainly comfortable vibe that belied his grouching. But, *mercy*, the two of them together were breathtaking. They had the same hair color and build, and together, they had quite a few appreciative looks being thrown their way. If the other brother was anything like that...

"Good looks run in the family, I see."

"Oh, they all look like that. You just have to get used to it. Hell on the ego, though, to have to stand next to them." Lily waved a hand, but the smile showed she was actually quite pleased with her husband's looks. "The whole family belongs on billboards. It's just dangerous and wrong for men to be so pretty."

It was a half-hearted grumble, and Caitlyn laughed. "I agree. Very disconcerting for the female population." Since Lily wasn't just any extra, Caitlyn indicated the chair next to her. "Would you like to sit?"

Lily shook her head. "I didn't really mean to disturb you that much. I just wanted to say that I was a fan. Not just your movies, either," she corrected. "I saw you do *Othello* in London. You were amazing. It made me cry."

"Thank you." There was something sincere and genuine about Lily that made her easy to talk to. "But please sit. It gets boring by myself sometimes, and I could use some company today." As Lily sat, Caitlyn asked, "How long have you been married to Ethan?"

"A little over a year. Brady—he's the oldest—got married last Christmas, so Finn's starting to feel the heat now."

Caitlyn nearly choked on her drink. Finn married? That was…well, simply unimaginable, regardless of how quickly the tabloids were to pre-plan any star's wedding. She had to assume that Finn's family would know that Naomi wasn't really in the running, but…*yikes*. Talk about stumbling into a minefield.

"Well, Finn tends to do…"

"Whatever he damn well pleases. Yeah, we know."

Exasperation and frustration tinged Lily's words. Maybe there was more danger here than she'd thought. Were there family tensions she didn't know about? He looked comfortable enough with his brother, but she knew all too well that looks could be deceiving. For Finn's sake, if nothing else, she didn't want to accidentally say anything that might make that worse.

She chose her words carefully. "You don't get along with Finn?"

Lily's eyes widened. "No! I mean, yes… I mean…" She shook her head. "I adore Finn. It's impossible *not* to."

"True." Caitlyn wanted to suck the word back once she saw the look on Lily's face. She reached for her drink. *Damn.*

"Is it difficult for you?" Her voice carried concern, not the digging-for-dirt she usually got. But this was Finn's sister-in-law…

She hedged her answer, anyway. "What do you mean?"

"Being here with Finn. Considering…"

Thankfully, she could fall back on the same pat answers she'd been using for weeks now. "We all have exes. And in this business, it's all but guaranteed you'll have to work with them at some point. You can't let all that personal stuff affect the work."

"I remember when you two were together. Just from the magazines, of course."

Great. She didn't realize she'd said it aloud until Lily laughed.

Patting her arm in a friendly and oddly comforting gesture, Lily said, "Believe me, I am the last person on earth who'd pass judgment on anyone for anything. I think that's why Finn and I get along. He's like that, too. As long as you're in a good place now, how you got there isn't important."

This must be the sister-in-law Finn had quoted at her with such admiration in his voice. An odd spurt of purely irrational jealousy spiked into her, but she forced it down. "You seem to know him pretty well."

"Finn was the only person to give me the benefit of the doubt when I needed it. I owe him big-time."

From the adoring looks Lily kept throwing her husband, that seemed slightly disloyal. "Not Ethan?"

"Since it was Ethan he was defending me against…" Once again she waved it away. "It's a long story. But Finn is special and I would like to see him happy."

Caitlyn's heart gave an odd stutter. "I think he is."

"Special? Or happy?" Lily challenged.

Caitlyn couldn't figure out the correct answer. "Both?"

Lily gave her a look that clearly questioned her sanity. "He's come a long way, but he has a way to go yet. Finn does a good job putting on the public face, but then all the Marshalls do. It worries me, though, and since you know him pretty well you probably know what I mean."

"I'm not sure we're on the same page. Finn and I aren't exactly—"

Lily kept on talking over Caitlyn's words, and Caitlyn realized that Lily probably knew Naomi wasn't really in the picture. Even worse, she'd jumped to the assumption that Caitlyn *was*.

"I think Finn's missing out on something, don't you? He's sheltered himself so long that I'm afraid that it's becoming the truth…"

Lily trailed off, and Caitlyn figured it had to have something to do with the confusion on her face.

"Or not."

Caitlyn wanted to press the issue more because, frankly, she was quite interested in this glimpse into Finn's psyche by someone who knew him well and wasn't romantically interested in him. But that would be out of line. It wasn't her business. And she had the sinking feeling she'd already revealed more than she should have to this woman.

Before she could regroup, though, someone called Lily's name, and she looked up to see Ethan motioning to his wife.

"I gotta run before I get in trouble. We had long lectures this morning about how we're not supposed to bother the stars. I was just so curious about you."

That statement seemed loaded and dangerous.

Lily slid off her chair. "I'm sorry if I bothered you, but it was very nice meeting you, Caitlyn. I hope to see you again."

"Me, too, Lily." It was unlikely, however, and Caitlyn felt a little twinge about that.

Lily went to her husband's side and he hauled her against him without pausing. It was lovely to see how attuned he was to Lily. Caitlyn could see some conversation go back and forth—and at least some of it was about her, since they occasionally glanced in her direction—before Finn frowned at Lily and Ethan shoved him. Laughter followed.

She put her headphones back on and went back to the script she was reviewing for later. The changes were minor, but she didn't want to hold anything up by not being on top of it. A minute later, though, she sneaked a peek at Finn, who had now moved to a table with Lily and Ethan.

It was interesting to watch, and she told herself her need to see was just research for future roles where she had a sibling and needed to create that family dynamic.

Lily was nice enough, but she was obviously wrong. Finn was possibly the happiest, most untroubled person she knew. He was certainly the most confident. Anything that wasn't great just got shrugged off those broad shoulders.

She sneaked another peek at Finn. So why wouldn't Finn be happy?

He had everything.

CHAPTER EIGHT

THE loud bangs on his front door coupled with the ringing phone he'd tried to ignore could only equal one thing. Well, two, actually: Brady and Ethan.

Finn glanced at the clock as he rolled out of bed and grabbed the jeans he'd left on the floor after another late night with Cait. She might have the morning off to laze about and catch up on sleep, but he didn't. Of course when he'd dragged his carcass home like some teenager sneaking in in the wee hours of the morning, he hadn't expected his brothers to come pounding on his door just after sunrise, either.

He stretched and felt his muscles protest. He and Cait were going to have to work on actually making it to a bed. The pounding got louder as he got closer, and he could hear the two of them outside his door. Sadly, there was zero chance they'd go away, so he had no choice but to answer.

Wrenching open the door, he squinted at the light and his annoying brothers. "What do you want?"

Brady held out a cup of coffee from the shop about two blocks away. "We are taking the ladies to Cherry Hill Park today for an art something-or-another, and they thought you might like to come along."

"No." Finn started to close the door in their grinning faces, but Ethan caught it and they both walked in as if they owned the place. He rolled his eyes but accepted the coffee when Brady held it out again.

"Why not?" Ethan asked.

"Because I don't want to."

That earned him a snort from Brady. "Neither do we, you know."

"The fate of the married man is to attend art shows for no reason at all. That's your bad luck."

Ethan dropped to the couch and propped his feet up on the coffee table. Brady took the chair opposite. It looked as if they planned to stay a while, and any hope of a return to bed was disappearing fast.

"Where are Aspyn and Lily? I thought you were—"

"Shopping," Brady answered. "There's a maternity store next to the coffee shop. They'll meet us here when they're done."

He never should have given any of them the address of his temporary home. He took the other end of the couch and scrubbed his face to wake up. "So you're just going to bother me until then?"

Brady took mock offense. "So much for brotherly love. We've barely seen you since you got back."

He pointed at Ethan. "I saw you yesterday." Turning to Brady, he added, "And I'll see you day after tomorrow."

"That's on the set. That's not what we meant."

"I'm not on vacation here. I'm working, remember?"

Brady snorted and pulled a magazine out of his back pocket. A picture of him and Naomi took up a good portion of the cover. "Could have fooled me. That doesn't look like work."

Finn left it where it landed. "Obviously you've never taken Naomi Harte to dinner."

"Trouble in paradise?"

"That was most definitely work by every possible definition of the word. You two are both well aware that certain things must be done for the sake of appearances, and letting people speculate about the nature of my and Naomi's relationship is good for appearances. There's nothing more to it than that."

Ethan looked at Brady. "You owe me fifty dollars."

More betting? When had his family become such gamblers? And on his personal business, no less. It was ridiculous.

But Brady wasn't paying. "No, you're only half there."

"Are you kidding me? I was there yesterday. There's a reason why our baby brother makes his living behind the cameras—he has no acting ability at all. Even Lily noticed you could've roasted marshmallows on the looks he was giving her."

Brady shook his head. "That doesn't mean the feelings are mutual."

"Oh, they're mutual. Caitlyn is not as transparent as this one, but—"

Finn started to interrupt, but his brothers seemed to have forgotten he was even in the room.

"Then why hasn't it leaked to the press?" Brady countered, indicating the magazine.

"Finn must have better control over his people than others do. Or else he just hires blind idiots to work for him—"

Finn stood and headed toward the bedroom.

"Where are you going?" Ethan interrupted himself to ask.

"You two don't seem to need me for this conversation, so…"

Ethan waved him back. "You could end it—and make me fifty bucks—by just 'fessing up that you're sleeping with Caitlyn Reese again."

"You don't need another fifty bucks."

Ethan merely grinned. "Ah, but the bragging rights that come with it are priceless."

Brady ignored Ethan to pin Finn with the "big brother" look and tone. "Not too long ago you were swearing that you and Caitlyn were ancient history, so your attempts to skate around the topic now make me think there is something going on between you two."

Ethan nodded. "Might as well tell us, because we're not going to let it rest until you do. I might even have to hint to Nana that—"

"Enough. Sometimes I wish I was an only child."

Brady nodded. "I think the same thing every day."

He'd never been one to care what anyone—including his brothers—thought of his love life, but for some reason he really didn't feel like sharing in this instance. Letting his brothers in to this part of his life just didn't sit right. It was what it was: two people who understood each other and their needs. But there was no way that those two idiots would let it rest, and unless he wanted to be hounded endlessly he had to tell them *something*.

"Cait and I are friends."

Ethan shook his head. "Try again. You've never been just friends with a woman."

"I didn't say we were *just* friends." He suddenly felt like a teenager. "We're close friends."

"Very close?" Brady asked.

He let the silence spin out, but his brothers didn't take the hint. "Quite close," he conceded.

Brady frowned and fished out his wallet. He handed a bill to Ethan, who pocketed it with a victorious grin, then turned that frown on Finn. "You do realize you're playing with fire here and just asking to burn the whole house down, right?"

"Wow, that's a tad over-dramatic. I am not now nor will I

ever be running for office, so even the biggest scandal I could possibly hatch won't bring down my career."

"Do you really give that little of a damn about other people?"

The heat in Brady's voice surprised him. "Excuse me?"

"It's not all about you, you know."

I never should have let them in. "I think the Marshall legacy will be fine, regardless of what I do."

"Probably. But I was talking about Caitlyn Reese."

"Cait is none of your business."

"And she shouldn't be yours, either. Aspyn brought me up to speed on Caitlyn's side of that sorry story. No wonder she's been in exile."

"What?"

"I only pay attention to you and your messes and how they affect us, so I'd never given a second thought to the fallout for her."

"She seems nice enough," Ethan added, "but I have to question her intelligence, getting mixed up with you again."

With that Ethan had crossed the line *and* reached the limits of Finn's patience in one fell swoop. "And that's all for today, folks. I need to actually work—and don't you two have an art show to go to?"

"Not just yet. We haven't said what we came to say."

"What is with you two this morning?" When Ethan merely raised an eyebrow, Finn got his answer. "Nana. She set you two on me, didn't she?"

"You haven't been out to Hill Chase recently."

"So she sent you two to lecture me on her behalf?" The need to hit something made his knuckles itch.

Ethan chuckled. "Something like that."

"And you people wonder why I live on the other side of the continent."

"We don't wonder at all," Brady said. "In fact, I'm often tempted to join you there."

"If that's supposed to be a threat, it's an empty one. You go into political withdrawal if you get more than a hundred miles from D.C."

"And you get downright belligerent at less than that distance." That remark came from Ethan.

"Because my family conspires to drive me insane."

"It's only because we care, you know," Brady countered.

"Then can we schedule this intervention for another day? Maybe one where I don't have an entire crew waiting on me to show up and actually work?" As if on cue, Finn's phone chimed as a text came in. He pounced on it gratefully. "Duty calls. I'll let you show yourselves out."

"You can't avoid this forever, you know."

Watch me.

Brady narrowed his eyes as if he'd actually heard Finn say the words. "Are you really that shallow? You're dating one woman in public for appearances' sake, sleeping with another on the side—I won't even go into the fact she's your ex—and you don't see a problem with that? Much less the fact that you're practically channeling your fath—?"

Finn held up a hand. "Stop. I don't know when you two decided to take up armchair psychology as a hobby, but you suck at it. I live in L.A., for God's sake, where everyone is in therapy."

Ethan shook his head. "God, you're grouchy today."

"Oh, gee, and it has nothing to do with being ambushed by my idiot brothers wanting to uncover my deep emotional problems before I'm even fully awake."

Brady turned to Ethan and shrugged. "At least he admits he has emotional problems. It's a step in the right direction."

"You two might be living an examined life these days, but it doesn't mean I have to. Not everything has to be tracked back to a childhood trauma and 'healed.' Quit dumping your daddy issues on me. The bastard has nothing to do with me or my life. He never has."

"And there's *your* problem."

"No, that's *your* problem. My problem is you two."

"And Cait," Ethan added.

Only the sound of his doorbell kept Finn from going for Ethan's throat. He'd never been quite so glad to have his sisters-in-law arrive. "I'm going to go take a shower. Lock the door behind you, okay?" He left them sitting in his living room with the sincere hope they'd be gone by the time he finished in the shower. This was *not* the best way to start his day.

The pounding hot water soothed his muscles but not his mood. *Why* did his brothers have to make something out of nothing? Especially something that was none of their business, like Cait. The thought of her calmed his temper some. While Cait might be guilty of self-examination these days, too, at least she didn't try to make her hang-ups his. She might be hard on herself, but she was easy on others, thank God. Brady and Ethan—and Nana, too—could use a few lessons from her on that.

He took a deep breath and calmed himself. This was temporary. Once he went home and wasn't quite so underfoot, his brothers and the Grands would back off. His life would go back to normal, and without Cait to fuel their ridiculous outrage they'd lose steam. They might continue to shake their heads and grumble, but two thousand miles would blunt the force.

All of this would pass. Normalcy was only a few weeks away.

Why, then, didn't the thought improve his mood?

A morning off was bliss. Caitlyn slept late, then went for a massage and a manicure. After a little shopping, where a few folks recognized her and asked for pictures, she went to the set for a couple of hours. Five minutes after she arrived, she was warned that Finn was being uncharacteristically grouchy, and one look at his face convinced her to keep her distance.

It was a short, easy day for her, but Finn's bad mood had rubbed off even though he'd barely spoken three words to her. She'd rather been hoping he might come by tonight, but that didn't seem likely, and it bothered her more than it should.

She'd given Finn an out, but he hadn't taken it. In fact, he didn't seem to mind the fact that she was all but using him. She didn't like herself much for doing it, but she couldn't seem to bring herself to give up this chance. It wasn't as if she could have a fling with Finn in L.A. Not with the paparazzi and star stalkers there. Thankfully, what passed for paparazzi in Baltimore wasn't exactly tenacious or on every street corner. She might as well enjoy this moment while she could. Even though it looked like she'd not be enjoying it tonight.

Caitlyn forced herself to shake off the disappointment. She had no claim on him, and there were no guarantees— not even short-term ones. It was none of her business where Finn was when he wasn't with her.

She just needed to keep that foremost in mind.

At seven o'clock that night Caitlyn tuned in to *The Catner Report*, which was tabloid cable TV at its sleaziest. As much as she hated the show, it would give her a good reading on the level of gossip surrounding her—if any—and get her up to speed on what was going on in the wider entertainment world.

Carrie Catner always led with the biggest scandals, and when her name didn't come before the first commercial break Caitlyn began to breathe easy. She felt a little sorry for Cindy Burke, who grabbed the headlines by checking into rehab yesterday. They'd done a film together seven or so years ago, and Cindy was actually a sweet girl and really talented—if a little troubled. At the same time it was fortunate Cindy didn't have her act completely together or else *she* wouldn't have the fantastic part of Rebecca. She didn't want to take pleasure at someone else's misfortune, but it had been a boon for her. She'd just have to deal with the guilt.

When her picture flashed on the screen after the commercial it wasn't unexpected—especially considering the tie-in to Cindy.

"Caitlyn Reese is a name we haven't heard much recently, but that seems set to change. Currently on location in Baltimore, Reese was a surprise addition to the all-star cast of *The Folly of the Fury* as a last-minute replacement for Cindy Burke. Reese made her name in a string of romantic comedies, then moved to London three years ago and worked in theater, only recently returning to the States for a brief—but successful—run on Broadway."

Way to damn with faint praise.

"But Reese is better known for her headline-grabbing affair with star producer Finn Marshall that played out, then flamed out, just prior to her London move. Many speculated the affair might have contributed to the move."

Well, that's not, too— Ugh! She stopped the thought as a clip of her and Finn on the red carpet was replaced with a picture of Finn doing a tequila shot out of her cleavage. *Where'd they get that one?* She had no memory of that event, but that wasn't surprising.

"Reese was spotted with her former flame at a fundraiser in D.C., spurring speculation that her return to the big screen might not be all business, but witnesses described the meeting as accidental and possibly antagonistic, even though Marshall's company is heading the project."

That was one way to put it.

"In an interesting twist, though, Reese and her co-star, heartthrob Jason Elkins, were spotted having a leisurely brunch at a Baltimore eatery amid a swirl of reports that the on-screen romance seemed almost too realistic. Meanwhile, Marshall has been seen escorting Naomi Harte, the film's leading lady, to several of Baltimore's best restaurants. Granted, Reese and Marshall may be over, but that's got to be one *interesting* set."

Carrie Catner grinned gleefully at the camera and Caitlyn felt herself snarl. *You don't know the half of it.*

"A spokesperson for the production company claims that Reese and Elkins are 'just friends,' but refused to comment on Marshall and Harte. I guess we'll just have to wait and see. *The Folly of the Fury* is scheduled to hit theaters next spring."

Caitlyn turned it off. Well, she and Jason had done their jobs, but it seemed strange that the company would be floating the truth in rumor form. And by not commenting on Finn and Naomi they were practically confirming a lie. *Interesting* wasn't the word she'd choose for it. Her life might carry soap opera potential, at least according to Carrie Catner, but that wasn't too bad. That one photo of her and Finn at some long-ago party wasn't flattering, but it wasn't the worst photo they could have used. *All and all, not too bad,* she decided.

Her phone chirped as a text came in, and Caitlyn had to dig through her bag to find it.

The message was from Finn: *"You busy?"*

The hopes she'd carefully kept tamped down leaped back up.

"No. Why?"

"Look out the window."

Okay, this was just a little weird. Why was he texting her instead of just calling? She went to the window and peeked through the slats of the blind. The street looked normal: just a few cars parked along the curb. Then, down to her right, she saw a flash. It happened again, and she realized it was the headlight of a motorcycle parked just beyond the streetlight. The rider was draped in shadow and his helmet obscured his features, but she recognized both the bike and Finn's broad shoulders. She could see the glow of the phone's screen as Finn typed another message. What on earth was going on?

The answer pinged to her phone almost immediately: *"Want to go for a ride?"*

Was he kidding? They hadn't been caught together yet off-set, but that would be just asking for trouble. The only reason he could come here at all was because several of the cast and crew—including the director—were living in this block of condos. If he were spotted entering the courtyard it could be brushed off as visiting any number of people.

"Are you crazy?"

"It's a nice night. Perfect for a ride."

She and Finn had used to ride down to Santa Monica or Venice Beach on nights like this. Memories rose up to greet her, but she shook them away. Sex was one thing. This tee-tered dangerously on the edge of Something Else. The fact that she *wanted* to go only confirmed it was probably a very bad idea.

Finn's next message seemed to read her mind: *"You know you want to."*

That was completely beside the point. *"No way. Too dangerous."* "Dangerous" could be interpreted many different ways, so that wasn't a lie.

"Why not?"

Argh. She needed a good excuse. *"Someone might see us."*

"Lame excuse."

She happened to agree, but it was the best she could come up with.

"But true."

"No cameras watching now."

That much was true.

Finn didn't wait for her to reply. *"Come on."*

She dithered, fighting the part of her that really wanted to go. Not just because it was Finn—as if that wasn't enough—but because this spoke to that adventurous part of herself she'd been keeping a tight lid on. If she took that lid off, even just for one night, would she be able to get it back on? And she now knew why Finn was texting instead of calling. He understood how to build drama and tension, and the texts added to that sense of adventure.

Her phone beeped again: *"Well? You coming?"*

No, she told herself. She wasn't going to go. She needed to keep things with Finn behind very clear borders. But she'd already slipped her feet into her shoes and found her hoodie.

"I'm absolutely insane," she said aloud as she grabbed her keys and bolted down the stairs.

Finn flipped up the visor to his helmet and grinned as she approached. "I knew you'd come." He held out a helmet to her.

"This is crazy." But she was already braiding her hair and tucking it down the back of her shirt.

The helmet went on easily and smelled brand-new, making her wonder when Finn had come up with this idea. He helped her fasten the chin strap and flipped down the visor, then revved the motor as she swung a leg over and got on behind him. Her thighs fit around his perfectly, and as she clasped her hands around his waist, her whole body seemed to sigh into him.

With a roar of the powerful engine, Finn pulled out into the street.

She hadn't asked where they were going, but honestly she didn't really care. Finn had that effect on her. And after three years of very studiously *not* getting onto the backs of motorcycles with men like Finn, this small act was enough to make her feel wholly alive for the first time in a long time.

Of course there weren't any other men like Finn.

She laid her head against Finn's back and closed her eyes, enjoying the feel of him and the sway of the bike and the rush of the air. The sensation immediately took her back in time.

When Finn stopped at a red light and one hand came back to rub along the outside of her thigh, it literally felt like old times.

Caitlyn lost track of how long they rode, but she wasn't concerned. Everything just felt right at the moment, and she wanted to enjoy it. She knew they were getting a distance from the city as the streetlights got farther apart and the smells of the city disappeared. Finn finally pulled off the side of the road to a stop.

She sat up and flipped up her visor as he killed the engine. "Where are we?"

"Out in the county. Look."

She followed his finger and saw the bright lights. She did a double-take. "Are those fairgrounds?"

Finn grinned at her, obviously pleased with himself. "Yep. I thought you might like to go."

She didn't remember ever telling Finn about going to the fair with her cousins during those summers when she was young, but the chances of this being a coincidence were just too astronomical. The fact Finn even remembered something as silly and unimportant as that warmed her. It was sweet, actually, but…

"We can't go wandering through the fair. Someone might see us there."

Finn shook his head. "You worry way too much. No one expects either one of us to be here, so they won't be looking. Even if they think we look familiar they'll be hard-pressed to place us. We'll be just another couple enjoying the fair. Anyway," he said, as a sly grin crossed his face, "I happen to know that Naomi made a huge deal about exploring Baltimore nightlife today in front of the people most likely to spread the news. Anyone who might be looking for either of us will be trailing after Naomi instead."

It wasn't just the fear of photographers, but that excuse still served nicely. "But still..."

"I know. That hair of yours is pretty distinctive. So I snagged this—" he reached into the small storage compartment "—from the makeup trailer."

A blond wig. "How original." She frowned at it. "Even if they don't recognize me, surely someone will recognize you. You're not exactly Mr. Low-Profile."

He shook his head. "In D.C. or L.A., maybe. At a county fair in the middle of nowhere Maryland? Not likely. Anyway," he produced something else from the compartment, "I brought a hat for me." He ran a hand over the stubble on his chin and cheeks. "And I didn't shave, either. We'll blend."

If Finn hadn't shaved, did that mean this was a planned event, not just something he'd come up with spur-of-the-moment? If so... She couldn't go there.

"I don't know..."

There were a dozen dangers lurking here, not the least of which was if they *were* spotted, Carrie Catner and her Report would have a field day.

His voice turned coaxing. "I'll buy you a funnel cake. Maybe even an ice cream cone, too, if you're really nice to me."

The temptation was extreme, but it had nothing to do with the promise of food. "Fine. If this backfires, though..."

"You can kill me." The grin said he wasn't the least bit worried either way.

"As long as we're clear on that." She took off her helmet and let Finn help her adjust the wig. The blond bangs fell to her eyebrows, but a look in the side mirror had her groaning. "I still look like me. Only as a blonde."

"But no one is looking for you." He cocked his head and studied her. "I prefer you as a redhead, though."

The helmet didn't fit quite as well over the wig, but it wasn't much farther to the fairground parking lot. Caitlyn mentally crossed her fingers as they joined the line at the ticket window.

She held her breath, but no one seemed to spare them a second glance. Most of the crowd was made up of teenagers, who were far too interested in their own groups to pay attention to two adults.

Finn had the brim of his ball cap pulled low over his eyes as he bought their tickets, and after several more minutes of winding through the crowd where no one seemed to even notice them, she began to relax into the sights and sounds and smells.

"So, is it like you remember?"

"Yes and no. I would have been about fifteen the last time." Once she'd turned sixteen and had outgrown a little of her teenage awkwardness, she'd started working more and quit spending summers with her aunt. "What about you?"

Finn shook his head as he bought an enormous cotton candy and handed it to her. "I've never been to one."

She pulled off a hunk of the spun sugar before offering it to him. "Ever?"

"Nope," he said around a mouthful. "Wait—I take that back. We stopped at a fairground during one of my grandfather's campaigns. I didn't really have much exploration time, though."

She understood that. How many places had she been with her parents without actually seeing them? "I'm sorry to hear that."

"Geez, Cait, you make it sound like I was deprived somehow."

"Maybe you were." Her childhood had been pretty screwed

up, but she'd had some periods that resembled a normal life—like the summers spent in Oklahoma. It had been the one upside to her parents' schedules. She hadn't appreciated it at the time, but in retrospect…

"Then you are the only person in the world to think my childhood was deprived in any way."

He said it with a laugh, but it brought another memory to mind. Finn's childhood had been really screwed up. Her parents were paragons compared to his, and he only spoke of them in passing, if at all. It was a touchy subject for him, and one she knew to stay away from. "If you never even went to a fair, maybe it was."

"My grandparents set one up in the grounds at Hill Chase for my tenth birthday party. There was a small Ferris wheel and a carousel. Does that count?"

Since her parents had done something similar, she could honestly say, "No, I don't think that counts. For a kid, the fair is all about the rides and the junk food, but for a teenager, it's a social experience. It's all about the boys."

That made him laugh. "Then I'm glad I missed out on that. I wasn't much interested in boys. Still not, ya know."

She tucked her hand under his arm and leaned in. "Look around. You can practically see the hormones in the air. The boys and girls travel in separate packs at first, but they'll start mingling soon enough. The girls are already hoping the right boy will ask to ride through the Tunnel of Love with them."

"That *would* hold appeal."

"And the boys will show off at the midway games to win the girls giant teddy bears. It's a very complicated and important part of adolescence."

Finn snorted. "A couple of summers spent in middle America and you're an expert on teenage courtship rituals?"

She straightened her shoulders and said primly, "The most

successful actors will look back and realize they have always been avid students of human experience."

An eyebrow went up. "Quoting your mother is cheating."

She rolled her eyes at him and sighed. "Fine. I was a teenage girl and there were cute boys around. I wanted to fit in and be like everyone else, so…"

He looked at her oddly. "But you weren't like everyone else."

"No, but I wanted to be." She struggled for the right words. "You know what it's like."

"No, I don't."

It took her a second to realize that Finn was serious. "You're telling me that you always advertised your pedigree to impress people?" Finn's unrepentant grin made her want to smack him. "You should be ashamed."

"Teenage boys feel no shame when it comes to pretty girls. We're slaves to our hormones and will do whatever it takes."

"And you never wanted anyone to just like you for you? Not because of your family?"

"Liking me for myself wasn't high on my list of priorities when it came to girls."

"That's truly shameful, Finn."

"Money and power are very attractive. You know that."

"I do. Which is why most people with money and power want to be liked for something else. They try to bring attention to their other qualities."

"But *not* teenage boys. I had no problem working that angle. Most people—regardless of age—are quite shallow."

"Well, I can't claim to be the deepest puddle there is, but that's not why I was interested in you."

"I know." His mouth twitched. "The first woman I'd met on either coast who didn't need my money or my connections."

She laughed. "Because I had my own, thank you very much."

"Exactly. That's why you were such a challenge."

"Me? A challenge?" She'd been swamped by his charm and looks and...*everything*. Finn was a force of nature, and she hadn't exactly played hard to get. *Then or now.*

"Definitely. It meant I had to actually talk to you about something, try to find common interests..." He trailed off with a shudder. "It was very difficult."

"I'm flattered."

He grinned. "You should be."

She smacked his arm half-heartedly, but the truth was that she *was*. In her world, it was often difficult to know what was real. In retrospect, though, she was beginning to realize that the Finn she'd known had been very different from the public Finn. The intervening years and layers of hurt had clouded that.

But it was heartening to see that Finn again. It was more than just flattering.

"And," Finn continued, "since you *still* aren't impressed by my money or my name, I'm now going to have to try to impress you your way." He sighed dramatically before twining his fingers through hers and leading her to the shooting gallery. "Which one of those teddy bears do you want?"

At that, this adventure seemed to morph into something that felt a lot like a date.

And it scared her more than a little.

But it wasn't nearly as scary as the feeling that washed over her when Finn finally won the fuzzy purple bear she'd pointed out. He presented it to her with flair, and her heart lurched painfully in her chest.

This was what falling in love with Finn Marshall felt like. She remembered it all too well. And that was dangerous.

CHAPTER NINE

Finn could have purchased a dozen teddy bears for the money he'd spent shooting an air rifle with a crooked sight at a stupid mechanical duck. But in the end, he'd prevailed, and Cait accepted the token with what he could only call glee. He'd seen women less appreciative of diamond jewelry.

"You can add it to your collection."

"Collection? Hardly. This is the first time anyone's ever won me one." She rose up on her tiptoes to kiss his cheek. "Thank you, Finn."

She seemed so genuinely pleased that Finn rather felt he'd accomplished something much more complicated—like dragon-slaying. He couldn't put a name on the feeling inside his chest, but he was very glad he'd decided to bring Cait here tonight.

Cait tucked the teddy into the crook of her elbow and dragged him toward something called the Scrambler. The ride looked decrepit and possibly unsafe—more like it belonged in a movie where dozens of people were about to be killed and maimed in an unfortunate carnival accident.

But Cait enjoyed it so much, they got back on for a second ride. The big surprise came when he realized he was enjoying it, too.

Cait, for all of her public glamour, was ridiculously easy to please. He'd forgotten about that. He'd forgotten how easy it was to just be with her, being Cait and Finn—not Caitlyn Reese and Finn Marshall. Cait couldn't be impressed or cowed by a famous name or a fat checkbook, and he didn't have to be anything other than himself.

Whatever reservations Cait had harbored earlier about being here evaporated completely as they made their way down the midway from ride to ride. As they reached the back gate Cait licked the last of the powdered sugar from her funnel cake off her fingers and looked around, the corners of her mouth turning down in a slight frown.

"What is it?"

"No Tunnel of Love. That stinks. I wanted to ride the Tunnel of Love."

A dozen cheesy *double-entendres* sprang to mind regarding tunnels of love, but he kept them behind his teeth. Mostly.

"You'll just have to fill me in later." But her disappointed frown only intensified. "What, Caity?"

"This was going to be my first time. I was looking forward to doing it."

"But earlier you said…"

"I said teddy-bear-to-Tunnel-of-Love was the general path. I never had a boy win me a bear *or* ask to ride the Tunnel of Love with me."

Oh, the need to say something about riding love tunnels was about to kill him. But Cait seemed genuinely disappointed. "Never? I find that very hard to believe."

"The part I didn't mention earlier was that I was a bit of a late bloomer, with a mouthful of braces and, geez, I thought I'd *never* get breasts. I was shy and awkward—particularly when I was so far out of my element—and I blended into the wallpaper. Without my pedigree on display I wasn't exactly Miss Popularity. Teenage boys can be quite shallow, you know."

She laughed, but it was slightly bitter. Obviously Cait's

experimental forays into being "normal" hadn't always been the way they worked out in the movies.

"This was going to be my do-over night. Rats."

As she sat on a nearby bench with a sigh, he had the urge to have a Tunnel of Love shipped in from wherever such things were made. He joined her on the bench. "I'm sorry."

"Don't be. I'm just being silly." She leaned back and toyed with the teddy bear. "As far as do-overs go, this was pretty awesome. I've had a great time. Thanks."

"My pleasure." And, surprisingly enough, he meant it.

"I need to tell you something."

"Okay."

"I was wrong to blame you for my problems. Then and now. I needed a bad guy—who wasn't me—and you were an easy target."

"We all do what we have to do to get through."

"Yeah, but I didn't handle it well. I thought I was fighting back, but I was really just running away. Going to London was just the literal part."

"Sometimes running away is the only way to handle something."

Cait started to say something, then stopped and bit her lip as she reconsidered. Finally she looked at him. "Like you did? You left Virginia and went to L.A."

"Pretty much."

"Do you ever regret it?"

"No. I needed to start over, away from my family and all the baggage that came with them. Do *you* regret it?"

"No." She gave him a half-smile. "The execution was a bit faulty, but overall I have no regrets."

"Good. Then accept it for what it is and move on."

"Like you do?"

"You can't change people who don't want to be changed. You can't change the past."

"So that's how you've come to peace with your fath— family," she corrected hastily. When he nodded, she laughed. "Wow, we really aren't normal people, are we?"

"Not even remotely."

That caused her to laugh again. "You know, *this* is probably the most normal thing we've ever done together—even if I include the wig. You're definitely the best-looking boy I've ever ridden on a Ferris wheel with."

Her hand landed on his thigh, and she squeezed gently. Cait's smile turned a little shy and knowing, but then she leaned in to kiss him. It wasn't the same kind of chaste kiss he'd received for the teddy bear, nor was it the hot, carnal kind that never failed to set him on fire. For lack of a better word, he'd have to call it "sweet."

At that moment Finn quit running. He and Cait made sense. They understood each other. He should have seen it years ago. He should have gone to London after her instead of trying to pretend she was just another ex. All his denials to the contrary were being proved false.

When she pulled away she looked happy and relaxed, and it transformed her face. He'd gotten used to the guarded, slightly wary look of mere tolerance she'd worn on the set for so long. This reminded him of the Cait he used to know, and he realized that even when they'd been alone recently she'd never really relaxed back into herself. Of course, they weren't exactly spending their time chatting, either. He brushed the blond bangs away from her eyes and ran a thumb across her jawline. Part of him wanted to take her back now and spend the rest of the evening in bed, putting a different kind of happy and relaxed look on her face—the sated kind. But he was oddly loath to end this. Hard on the heels of that realization came an even more shocking one. He was loath to end any of it, and *that* was the biggest shocker of all.

"Wanna ride the Ferris wheel again?"

She beamed. "Sure."

He stood and held out his hand. Cait tucked the teddy bear in the front pouch of her hoodie before she took it.

Three steps away from the bench, he heard someone shout "Finn!" He turned a split-second before he realized he shouldn't.

The flash of the cameras nearly blinded him.

The weatherman on the news predicted a near-perfect summer day of warm temperatures, low humidity and lots of sunshine—an ideal day to get outside and enjoy.

But there was no way in hell Cait could leave her house. She was trapped unless she wanted to face the cameras waiting outside. All the shades were drawn tightly shut, and only a visit from the police earlier this morning had kept the media confined to the sidewalk and street beyond.

Ah, for the good old days, when it took longer than twelve hours to break a story. Thanks to the internet, and the twenty-four-hour cable channels with plenty of time to fill, news spread like wildfire.

They'd sprinted out of the fair last night, but in the time it had taken them to get back to the city, the local paparazzi had been tipped off and were waiting for them outside her condo. She went and peeked out the window. *Yep, still there.*

The director was fit to be tied, gossip-hungry locusts had descended on the set, effectively shutting down production for the day. Her agent was hyperventilating. Jason Elkins was giving interviews denying that they'd ever been anything more than colleagues. Thank goodness she hadn't gone with the original idea to really snuggle up for the cameras, or today would have been very embarrassing for them both.

But the worst was Naomi, who'd appeared on TV looking beautifully woebegone, the occasional tear sliding down her cheek as she spoke of heartbreak and betrayal.

It was a disaster, and as soon as she got near Finn Marshall again she was going to kill him just as she'd promised.

Her only contact with Finn, though, had been a brief text telling her to *"sit tight."* She hadn't responded because she wasn't quite sure exactly what she wanted to say to him, and she didn't trust her temper not to say something she'd regret. Since she had no plans to run that gauntlet outside until she had a good story in place, that instruction had been unnecessary, anyway.

But it meant she was locked inside, unable *not* to watch the entertainment news shows. The rash of amateur cameramen who'd gotten Finn's attention and then followed them out of the fair hadn't been the first attention they'd drawn that evening, based on the photographic evidence. She'd let her guard down too soon, gotten caught up in the fun and forgotten to be careful. There was a picture of Finn winning the teddy bear, one of them climbing onto the roller coaster and—her personal favorite—one of them kissing on the bench.

Oddly enough, her disguise had worked; it was Finn who'd first drawn attention—the man had a bigger following than some A-list stars, for God's sake—so the first story to break had been about Finn "cheating" on Naomi with some unidentified woman.

Unfortunately it had been only a short jump to then identify the blonde.

That was when the fun had really started. And it was worse than she'd imagined. In addition to "cheating" on Jason—his protestations about their relationship were being chalked up to avoiding the shame of being cheated on—she was being painted as "the other woman" in Finn and Naomi's relationship. From the mileage being made out of that, you'd have thought Finn and Naomi were married with a couple of kids and she was a homewrecker.

And, of course, their history was being rehashed with glee

by the talking heads. And *where* had they found all those pictures? She didn't remember half of them—which really wasn't surprising, as they'd tended to party hard back then and there were several nights that were fuzzy at best. It was embarrassing, but Finn had been right about one thing: she'd been far too skinny.

She and Finn making out in the back of a limo. Finn giving her a piggyback ride out of a club—she had her shoes in one hand and her hair was a mess. There were the ones she called the "Sunset Series": three photos of her stumbling off a curb and sprawled on the ground, two of Finn swinging at the cameraman and one of them arguing with the police. *Classy.* Someone had finally dragged out the one of her on Finn's motorcycle, and her humiliation was complete.

She would never claim that their reputations were completely undeserved—but, geez, no wonder it had got as bad as it had. In the retrospective pieces on TV they both looked as if they were one bender away from celebrity rehab.

Especially her. And while there were plenty of stories of the young and famous shaving their heads, forgoing underwear when climbing out of cars and wearing electronic anklets for multiple DUIs to compete with her flame-out, somehow *she* seemed to be the poster child for all that was wrong with "Kids in Hollywood."

She should turn it off, but listening to the reporters gleefully describe her fall from grace was exactly the punishment she deserved. Lord, the public never forgot anything. Even if they did, the gossip columns were happy to remind them.

She heard an increase in the noise level outside and went to the window. Peeking through the shades, she saw Finn making his way through the crowd, ignoring the shouted questions and waving away the cameras.

Nice of him to let me know he was coming by. Part of her was feeling petty enough to leave him standing out there to face the press and the ensuing embarrassment alone, but that would only make the situation worse. Instead, she unlocked the door and let him in.

She slammed the door behind him and threw the bolt. "You are a brave man to show up here, you know."

"They're just reporters."

She leaned against the door. "The press is *not* who you should be scared of at the moment."

"If you'll just calm down—"

His patronizing caused her to lose her already tenuous grip on her temper. "I will not calm down. I've spent all morning trapped in here—"

"I haven't exactly been at the beach myself. I've been trying to do damage control."

"This is your idea of damage control?" She waved at the TV, where they were replaying Naomi's and Jason's clips. "It looks more like every man for himself right now. Why aren't *they* 'sitting tight'?"

"It's messy, yes, but—"

She gritted her teeth. "Just once in your life could you at least pretend to give a damn about something? Anything?"

Finn finally got irritated and lost that calm, placating tone. "If you'd lay off your pity party for just a minute," he snapped, "I'll explain how we're going to get through this mess. All of us."

"Oh, I'm all ears." She stomped over to the couch, so mad now that she was tempted to take a swing at him. The pictures flashing on the screen now—what she was beginning to call their worst hits—didn't help her mood any. She pointed at the TV. "*That* was exactly what I wanted to avoid. I was very clear about not wanting my past with you dragged out and rehashed."

"Then you shouldn't have signed on to one of my projects."

"Excuse me?"

He crossed his arms over his chest. "Not everything is about you, Cait. Your insistence that everyone try to pretend we had no past helped put us in this position."

"You're blaming *me*?" Her head might explode at any moment.

"Oh, I've saved some blame for Naomi, too, because her unreasonable demands based on her jealousy of you caused part of this, but you get your fair share."

"And you get none at all? How convenient. My apologies for coming by your apartment and your trailer—"

"Enough. I won't apologize for wanting you. I've never hidden that fact and, you're right, I don't give a damn who knows it."

"You've made that very clear," she muttered.

He continued as if he hadn't heard her. "But I have bigger issues to deal with."

"I don't know. This seems like a pretty big deal to me."

"And you're right. It seems like a big deal. To *you*."

At that moment she almost hated him. And it hurt. But that hurt was a vivid reminder of why she should have never abandoned her earlier plan not to get near him again.

"In the grand scheme of things, Caity, it's not, and it will blow over. Hollywood is nothing if not forgiving."

Caitlyn opened her mouth to argue, but Finn cut her off.

"I will not let this mess derail my project at this point. Go on camera and say whatever you want to make yourself feel better. Say we're just friends, or that you were trying to steal me away from Naomi. I don't really care. Just say something and be ready to stick by it. But think carefully about what you want to say, because you'll have to ride out whatever comes after that."

"In other words, you're not going to involve yourself? How typical of you to just remove yourself from the situation. It gives me the choice of either getting pulled into a catfight with Naomi over you or falling on my sword. Great." She collapsed back with a sigh and rubbed her hands over her eyes.

"You're overreacting. I'd recommend you take the middle path and just let it blow itself out. You only have four days of filming left before the rest of us go back to L.A. to finish up. You can suck it up for that long."

She pushed to her feet and started to pace. "Gee, Finn, thanks for the support."

"Frankly, I've had it with the whole damn lot of you. The pettiness, the egos…"

"*My* ego? You're practically asking me to wear the scarlet letter for the sake of *your* project and you have the nerve to complain about *my* ego in the same breath?"

"You're damn right. Big picture time, Cait. The project is what matters here."

"To *you*." She threw his words back at him.

"It should matter to you, too. You of all people—"

That stopped her pacing. She stepped in front of him. "Me of *all people?*"

"Your father is famous for saying it's all about the work, not the people. You know that's how it works."

"Do *not* quote my parents to me. I'm well aware what they say in public. Unlike you, though, I know what they say in private. And my father told me many times that starlets are infinitely replaceable. Why do you think—?" She interrupted herself. "Oh, that's right. You don't think about anything other than yourself."

"Says the person too focused on her own press to realize that if she'd focus on *Folly* instead of—"

He knew just where to aim the blows to do the most damage to her ego. Well, so did she. "Screw you, Finn. This isn't about the damn film. Your precious picture will be fine. Your grandparents will be so proud, and you'll outshine your brothers for once. Hip, hip, hooray."

His eyes narrowed. "Don't bring my family into this."

"Why not? You brought mine into it."

"Because it was relevant."

"Here's relevance for you. Go to hell."

"Oh, grow up, Cait. This kind of garbage just comes with the territory."

"No, this kind of garbage comes from being with *you*. Once again I'm getting dragged down, and you won't lift a finger to help." There—she'd said it. It had been simmering under her anger all day.

"I am trying to help."

"Lord, I'd hate to see what you do when you do nothing. Oh, wait—I already know. Maybe I should just pack my bags and head back to London."

"Don't play the martyr, Cait."

"I'll play whatever part I damn well want. It's well within my range. Rest assured, though, that I'll make sure that *Folly* is everything you want it be. Can't let your grandparents down again, can we?"

"Well, just realize that there's no project in the world that will make your parents proud enough to actually pay attention to you."

She saw red and heard the slap reverberate around the room. Only when the painful sting started crawling over her palm and up her arm did she realize she'd actually slapped him. It had been hard enough to turn his head, and his cheek was turning red from the impact. She'd never been mad enough to hit another person before. Guilt battled with the elation of vindication as the silence grew heavy between them.

Finn rubbed his fingers over the mark. "The A.D. will be in touch about call times tomorrow. After losing time today, we'll be rearranging the schedule."

Caitlyn was still breathing hard, and the anger and adrenaline rushing through her blood had her shaking. The sinking feeling in her stomach, though, came from something else entirely and bordered on pain.

"I'll be there."

A curt nod was Finn's only response, and he was out the door before she could say anything else. She heard the shouts of the crowd outside, then the roar of Finn's motorcycle.

That hadn't gone as planned.

She went to the fridge in search of wine.

Five hours later Caitlyn was comfortably buzzed, but it wasn't enough to take the pain away. In fact, it was simply making it easier to be depressed and cranky. She should have known better than to seek solace in a bottle again. It wasn't helping any more this time than it had in the past.

The throng outside her door had thinned a little, but not enough for her to brave going out. Not that she had anywhere to go.

And she didn't have anyone to call, either.

So instead she got to sit here, alone, and think. And thinking was the very last thing she really wanted to do, because the more she thought, the less she liked her conclusions.

Funny how everyone had used to say she was a happy drunk. Today she was just a maudlin drunk, steeping in her own pity.

Finn had been partly right. It galled her to admit it, and it disgusted her that she'd been so far off-base before as to not see it herself. She'd spent her whole life trying to prove something to her parents, and when that hadn't worked she'd bounced the other way and made sure she had their—and everyone else's—attention. From then on, it had just been a vicious circle.

Funnily enough, Finn was the only person who had genuinely seemed to accept her back then. She snorted. *Because he hadn't cared.*

But he had to have cared a little bit. Maybe? At least back then? Or not. It was very hard to tell because he cared about so little. Especially now, damn him.

She'd locked up all her inner parts to keep them safe and under control, and then she'd given the key to the last person on earth she should. Why on earth was she surprised to end up right back here again? It would have been insanity to expect a different result.

Caitlyn leaned back on the couch and closed her eyes. At least Finn was consistent. And he seemed happy enough. Maybe she should take his advice.

Why did she care what people said about her? The tabloids contained no truth at all, so why let it bother her? Why *not* just do as she damn well pleased and at least make herself happy?

Folly would guarantee her entry back into her career. It wasn't Finn who'd made her look like such a loose cannon that no one wanted to work with her. So as long as she kept the partying to a minimum she'd still have her job. The rest of it... Well, she'd just have to hold her head high and act like she didn't care.

It wasn't as if she didn't have a shining example to follow. Finn was certainly the master, and she could simply emulate him.

It had to be easier than this.

"Do you need me to find you a local dentist?"

Finn looked up to see Liz, one of the P.A.s, looking at him oddly. "No. Why?"

"You keep rubbing your jaw like it hurts or something. Do you have a toothache?"

"I'm fine." His jaw was a little sore. Who'd have known Cait had such a strong right arm? He fully admitted he'd deserved it, though; that crack about her parents had been uncalled for and he was honest enough to admit it. But her accusations and blame-throwing had pushed him to retaliate in kind, and he'd gone directly where he knew it would hurt most.

And he felt bad about it. That wasn't his style or usual M.O. He just hadn't decided how—or if—to apologize for it.

Because, honestly, he was still pretty damn angry over the entire mess. It had little or nothing to do with the media circus playing out around them; he'd spent his entire life jumping from one ring of the circus to another, and he knew that eventually the circus would pack its tents, move to another town and someone else would grab the spotlight.

Right now, he'd just like to finish this project with a minimum of headaches or disasters. That would be lovely.

It was also highly unlikely.

He was in an evil mood, and he felt bad about what happened at Caitlyn's the other night. He hadn't spoken to her since then, figuring they both needed some time to cool down. He still wasn't fully there and wouldn't be until he'd had a chance to sort out her warped thinking.

According to her, *everything* was *always* his fault. And her constant fall-back argument that he simply didn't care was growing old, not to mention insulting. If he didn't care about her he wouldn't have taken her to that stupid fair in the first damn place. Maybe going to the fair wasn't the best idea he'd ever had, but that didn't warrant him getting branded the villain *again*. Either she was unbelievably shallow or completely self-absorbed. Possibly both.

Evil wasn't a strong enough word for his mood, actually.

The crisp, disapproving email from Nana had just about pushed him right over the edge. His brothers he could ignore. Their calls went straight to voice mail to be deleted. The crew...they were professionals and would get the job done. The cast—well, they could just suck it up and act like adults.

Naomi was getting all the mileage out of this that she could, and Jason was just an idiot who could also be ignored. Nana, though, was not ignorable, and she had the irritating ability to make him feel like a naughty child.

She *was* avoidable, though, and for now he was avoiding both her email and voice mails. It wasn't as if she could get more upset over this "deplorable and embarrassing" situation.

Cait was also avoidable—and she was avoiding him—but that would soon change. A glance at the activity outside showed that the crew had broken for lunch, so he sent a text to Cait: *"Meet me in your trailer so we can talk."*

A reply came back a few minutes later. *"Now is not a good time."*

Finn was sorely tempted to text back *Tough*, but Cait's next message came through before he could.

"I have a long day ahead and talking to you now will only throw me off. I need to concentrate."

Had it been any other excuse he'd have searched her out at the catering trailer whether she liked it or not. But Cait was doing exactly what he'd asked her and everyone else to do: sucking it up and getting the job done.

She'd even made a statement to the media from the stairs of her condo: "Finn Marshall is a colleague and a friend, but that line got blurred the other night. We all know how dangerous trips down memory lane can be. My apologies go to Naomi for my behavior, but only she and Finn can decide where they will go from here. You can all be assured it was a one-time mistake. Now I'd just like to focus on finishing this film."

He'd told her he didn't care what she said, so why did that tick him off? Obviously he was just going to be in and stay in a foul mood all day.

At least until he got to talk to Caitlyn and get this sorted out.

CHAPTER TEN

HURRY up and wait. That was the mantra of all productions. Usually Cait didn't mind; she enjoyed watching the crew—the attention paid to every detail, the work that went into making the magic. The actors' parts in the production almost seemed superfluous sometimes, like an add-in at the last minute.

But today she had no patience for the hanging around. This was her last scene on her last day of filming. Unless something went wrong, or a problem was discovered at a later date, her part was done. And, while she felt some sadness at putting aside Rebecca and moving on, Caitlyn couldn't ignore the itching feeling between her shoulderblades. Freedom seemed just a short distance away.

The last two days had given her time to think, to focus on what she really wanted and what was really best in the long run. Now that she knew, she was ready to move on and put this behind her.

It was big talk—if slightly repetitive at this point—but she had a *real* plan now. Just because she was now on Plan Q because Plans A through P had gone up in flames, that didn't mean it wasn't a good plan, nonetheless.

She sat in her chair, waiting for the director to quit arguing with the script supervisor, and fiddled with her phone for lack of anything better to do. The upcoming scene would be a relatively easy one: awkward moments with Jason and

Naomi's characters and a stilted goodbye. It was perfect for her mood. It would barely count as acting.

When a shadow crossed over her she looked up with a start.

It was only Naomi, but the relief was short-lived. While she'd been avoiding Finn the last two days, she'd been tense because Finn might decide he wanted to talk, anyway—whether or not it would throw her off her game—but Naomi wasn't exactly who she wanted to talk to, either.

With a cold, smug smile, Naomi took the seat next to her. Caitlyn went back to her phone, determined to ignore her, regardless of how childish it might seem.

Naomi opened with a dramatic sigh. "Well, I hope you're happy, Caitlyn."

Pretending to misunderstand her meaning seemed the best idea. "I am." She forced herself to sound cheerful and relaxed. "It's been great working on this project, but I'm looking forward to having some time off."

Naomi's eyes narrowed. It wasn't a good look for her, especially with all the makeup she had on. "I meant, I hope you're happy that you've managed to make this entire production all about you."

The scold in her tone only raised Caitlyn's hackles. She wasn't in the mood for this. "I know what you meant, Naomi. I was just giving you the chance to *not* act like an immature bitch."

Naomi's jaw dropped slightly, but she recovered quickly. "I can be an immature bitch. It's one of the perks, you know. I'm America's Sweetheart at the moment, and you're just a has-been who can't keep her legs together around Finn Marshall."

So that's how it's going to be? Fine. "Stings, does it?" Sarcasm dripped off her words.

Eyes wide and innocent, Naomi played dumb. "What?"

"The fact he doesn't want you."

Naomi huffed. "At least I have some pride. Finn may want you, but he sure doesn't love you. Not then, not now. You're just a convenient playmate."

Naomi's words stung, but Caitlyn was a good enough actress not to let it show. "It still doesn't change the fact that, given the choice between me and you, he chose to play with me. Losing out to me again has got to suck."

Oh, she'd hit a nerve with that comment, but after a brief stutter Naomi shrugged. "Only if I really wanted him. Which I don't."

"Then you're a better actress than I gave you credit for. Because you're sure acting like you're jealous. Everyone—especially the press—thinks so."

"Better to be thought jealous than a drunk slut," she fired back.

Caitlyn pretended to consider the statement. "You're right. It's a bit of a bummer I spent all that time trying to rebuild my reputation only to come home and pick up right where I left off." Naomi started to smile at her seeming victory, so Caitlyn went in for the kill. "Unfortunately for you, though, I *am* home. And I'm here to stay. Even though every tabloid is dragging my name through the mud, at least they're spelling it right. 'America's Sweetheart' is just a nice way of saying 'pretty but boring.'"

Heat flashed in Naomi's eyes. "Big talk from the person who started this whole disaster just to try and make everyone forget what happened three years ago."

"That was my mistake. I should have been wearing my past proudly to show how far I've come. So, while I may have fumbled this pass, I guarantee I'll be doing my touchdown dance soon enough."

"You think you're that good? You actually think this will be the time you'll step out of your mother's shadow?"

"I *know* I'm that good. And if anyone's worried about shad-

ows, it's you. *I'm* not the one who had to get Finn to take me
on a couple of 'dates' in order to make sure no one forgot I
was working on this picture. And once it's released—"

"I'll have top billing," Naomi interrupted smugly.

"Well, there's a first—and a *last*," she emphasized, "time
for everything, isn't there?"

If it were possible, steam would be pouring out of Naomi's
ears. Caitlyn watched as Naomi clenched her fists and knew
she was itching to smack her. "Now who's being an immature bitch?" she snapped.

"Caitlyn? Naomi?"

Caitlyn looked up to see one of the P.A.s approaching with
a wary look. And it wasn't just any P.A.; Liz worked directly
for Finn. Her little snipe-fest with Naomi had not gone un-
noticed, and while Liz wouldn't spread tales unnecessarily,
it would definitely make it back to Finn.

She forced her face into a neutral smile. "Yes?"

"They're ready for you."

"Wonderful. Thank you." She stood and brushed at a wrin-
kle in her dress. She felt amazingly calm and centered, which
was odd since she should be all tangled up after that conversation. Naomi, however, looked as if her head was about to
explode. "Your face is a little red, Naomi. Maybe you should
go back to Makeup and see what they can do for you."

She left Naomi sputtering.

"I've never seen anything like it, Finn." Liz was wide-eyed as
she gave him the rundown on the showdown. "I mean, I was
expecting hair-pulling and scratching to start at any minute."

At least they'd waited until Cait's last day to get into it.
"Do you know what it was about?"

She shrugged. "Something about billing and bitchiness."

"Personally, I'm surprised they didn't go at it before now.
Did everything go okay after?"

Liz nodded. "Perfect, actually. They got it in one take. They're still finishing up with Jason, though."

"Good. We can wrap this up and go home. I've had enough of this place. How about you?"

"Definitely. It's so humid here." Liz slowed down as they approached the trailers. "I'll...um...go pack up some more stuff. I'm pretty sure Caitlyn's in her trailer."

Finn let her go ahead and angled off towards Cait's. Her door was standing open, and as he approached, a duffle bag landed at the bottom of the steps. He stepped over it and entered without knocking.

Cait seemed to be sorting through a stack of papers on the table. With a sigh, she just scooped them all up and shoved them in her backpack. When she stood and saw him she froze. Then she sighed again. "By all means, come on in."

The trailer was stripped of all personal items already. "You seem to be in a rush."

"I've been ready to go for two days now. I don't have much here, or at the condo so I'll be leaving in the morning."

"For New York or L.A.?"

"New York, actually." Her voice was falsely friendly. "I left so quickly that I left some things unfinished. Then I'm taking a short vacation, and I'll be back in L.A. in a couple of weeks. If you need me—for something *Folly*-related," she clarified, "my agent will know how to find me."

Cait was cold and distant, and all but telling him to forget her phone number. Her attitude hadn't improved over the last two days. But then, hadn't Cait already proved she could carry a grudge?

She zipped up the backpack and hiked it over her shoulder. "I would like to thank you and Dolby and Walter for this experience. It's been a great opportunity for me." She lifted her chin, seemingly proud of herself.

Since she wasn't going to bring it up, he was going to have to. "About the other day…"

Her shoulders dropped a fraction of an inch. "Yeah. I guess I should apologize for slapping you."

"You were stressed."

She snorted. "Don't make excuses for me, Finn. I said I *should*, I didn't say I was going to. You deserved it."

This was a change. He hadn't expected her to be so adversarial about it. He didn't know what he *had* expected, but whatever he'd planned to say escaped him now.

Her attitude changed and her voice became crisp and irritated. "Do you need something? I have a lot to do before I leave."

"I just wanted to see how you were holding up."

"Just fine." She smiled and lifted her chin, but the smile was plastic.

"You're a good actress, but even I'm not believing that."

"You're right. I'm not fine." Her face softened and, eyes downcast, she closed the space between them. "This is such a mess."

"It's blowing over already. By the time you get to L.A., something else will have taken its place."

"I was talking about us."

The sudden change threw him. And when her hand came up to rest on his chest and trace over his heart, the muscles twitched involuntarily.

"You know, I missed you so much when I left. I nearly called a dozen times."

Her voice was husky, longing, and it brought out a similar feeling in him. "Why didn't you?"

"It was hard, but I'd been kicked around so much by the press—and you were all tangled up in that—and I was hurting. I figured a clean break was best. You know, leave it all behind." Cait's voice was low, and her eyes followed her hand as it moved over his shoulder, his arm. "I thought I'd moved on, but I guess I'm a little like the media. Unable to forget." She fell silent, but her hands continued to move, stoking the fire. Finally, she spoke again. "Do you want to know why my love scenes with Jason were so hot? Because he wears the same aftershave you used to. I could smell it and picture you. Picture *us*."

His skin tightened.

"Some memories are just burned into your soul, you know? I thought I was over it, that I'd be able to resist, but I was wrong. I told myself I could have one small taste without danger. I was so wrong. You're my drug, Finn, and I simply can't resist. Even when I know it's bad for me. So it got me thinking..." She lifted her eyes to his then, and he nearly recoiled from the anger and bitterness there. Her hand came to his nape and she pulled him closer. "Why resist?"

He grabbed her shoulders and set her away from him. A smirk played at the corner of her mouth. "What the hell is wrong with you?"

"Nothing, Finn. I'm actually feeling quite right, and I owe that to you. So if you want one more for the road..." Her face was a picture of innocent confusion, but her words hit him with the same force her slap had. "What? Isn't that why you came here to see me? What you wanted?"

So much for understanding her. For thinking they somehow made sense together. He felt foolish, and he didn't like it. "Silly me. I came to check on you. I was worried."

"Ah. No need to worry about me." She moved away and perched on the edge of the table. "Why the face, Finn? I'm doing exactly what you told me to do. You've been right all along."

"About...?"

"Not giving a damn what other people think. It's very... liberating." There was something dangerous in her voice.

"I've always thought so."

"So I've decided to quit fighting it. Every town needs a bad girl who tries but never quite gets redeemed. It gives them someone to root for and feel superior about at the same time. I think I've found my niche."

He could see the anger and frustration radiating off her, but it was the determination that worried him. "What happened to your great redemption story?"

"Eh." She waved a hand. "I shouldn't try to play outside my range. People can tell when it's false. You certainly saw right through it. I hope you'll understand, though, when I say that we're kind of played out as well. I'm only looking to you for inspiration, not participation."

Finn didn't know what to say. He needed to say *something*, but this Cait seemed like an entirely different person, and he had no idea where to even begin with something that wouldn't make this entire farce even worse.

She seemed to be waiting for him to speak, and when he didn't, she pushed to her feet and rubbed her palms on her jeans. "So, I think that's a wrap. Are you here in your official capacity as producer?" She waited for him to shake his head. "And you're not here for sex, so I guess we're done."

Cait grabbed her backpack and slung it over her shoulder. "I'm sure I'll see you around."

"Cait…"

She sighed. "You've got some talent, Finn, but you're really not *that* good of an actor. Don't try to pretend you care. It's beyond your range."

Finn was speechless, and the feeling didn't sit well.

Caitlyn felt as if she was choking. Her throat felt closed and tight and it was nearly impossible to inhale. She'd been running on anger and outrage and frustration for days now, but the pain was finally starting to break through.

That had been the performance of her life. Definitely award-worthy. But, damn it, she would *not* let Finn toy with her like that.

She hadn't being lying, though, about the addiction. She'd been foolish enough to think that a taste of Finn would be safe. That she'd be able to put him behind her again.

She'd been horribly wrong. And the withdrawal symptoms were killing her. She loved the big jerk, but Finn wasn't capable of returning the feeling. Hadn't he proved that three years ago? Why had she gone and put herself back there again?

Because she was an idiot. A glutton for punishment. Even now, as much as she was hurting, she wanted him. If he hadn't pulled away, she'd have happily…

She had to give him some credit, though. Finn hadn't misled her; he'd been upfront from the start. He wasn't the one changing the rules mid-game and then crying when the other side didn't want to play.

No, this was her mess. Because the same things she hated about him were the same things she loved about him. The acceptance. The freedom. The lack of pretense. It was honest, but without more it felt shallow.

She laughed at herself. Oh, the irony. Looking for depth in Hollywood was a fool's errand. Unfortunately, after a lifetime in that puddle she really wanted something in her life that had some depth.

And Finn wasn't it.

Of course she had to accept the fact that maybe she wasn't that deep, either, and that bothered her. For now, at least. If it were true…well, she'd learn to accept it. Maybe embrace it even. It wasn't defeatist; she simply needed to find her strength and play to it. Even if there wasn't much to that strength.

With a sigh, she started the car and looked up to see Finn standing in the doorway of the trailer, watching her. It was impossible to read his face. Possibly there simply wasn't anything there to read.

She took a deep breath and was glad to feel the constriction in her throat loosen at bit as she realized she'd accomplished more than she thought.

She'd faced down Finn and survived, after all. She could face down Hollywood, too.

Finn tossed his cards on the table and Brady reached over to flip them faceup. When he saw Finn's hand, he sighed and nudged Ethan. "The idiot went all in on a pair of absolutely nothing."

Both his brothers looked at him as if he'd lost his mind. Finn shrugged.

Granddad's game room at Hill Chase was decorated to evoke old-fashioned gentlemen's clubs: dark woods, leather chairs, muted lighting. From the bar and dartboard at one end of the room to the pool table by the balcony doors, it was a masculine space, perfect for brotherly games of poker at the card table in the middle. The rest of the main house was quiet—the Grands, Lily and Aspyn had retired long ago, leaving them to beer and cards.

Brady had the "Disappointed Big Brother" look down pat. "Is there nothing sacred to you?"

"What? It's poker, Brady."

"Exactly. I thought you at least still took poker seriously."

He could happily punch Brady for that crack, but Nana disapproved of them destroying her furniture. At the same time, a knock-down-drag-out with his brothers might just make him feel better. He certainly wanted to hit something, but they'd wake the house if he did.

"It's just a game."

"Which I just won, by the way," Ethan reminded him, raking in the pot with glee.

Finn lifted his beer in a toast. "Good for you."

Ethan pushed back from the table and crossed his arms. "Okay, what the hell is wrong with you? Your mood is just… foul."

"Well, we can't all be a constant ray of sunshine like you."

Brady nearly spat his drink. When he recovered, he grabbed Finn's beer and moved it to the other side of the table. "I think it might be time to cut you off. You've obviously lost grip with reality."

"Hey, they call L.A. La-La Land for a reason. Reality isn't necessary."

Ethan looked at Brady and spoke as if Finn wasn't even at the table. "He *is* in bad shape."

Finn knew they weren't referring to the amount of alcohol he'd consumed. He was nowhere near done drinking them under the table. While none of them had mentioned their visit that other morning, he knew his brothers hadn't forgotten the topic entirely. He'd love to know what they reported back to Nana, though, because the lecture he'd expected had never come.

It was rather disturbing. Disturbing enough for him to broach the subject. "Am I a bastard?"

Brady snorted. "Well, I can't say with certainty, because I wasn't at your conception—thank God—but you do look a lot like the rest of us. So, I'll go with no."

"I should really know better than to try to converse with you two."

Ethan's face rearranged itself into honest curiosity. "Tell us what's on your mind, then, little brother. We're all ears."

He debated for a moment, then decided that if he could go all in on nothing once tonight, he might as well do it again. "Cait."

Ethan reached for his wallet and handed Brady a bill.

So much for thinking his brothers could be serious about

this. "Good God, what is it with y'all and this need to bet on my life?"

"It keeps us from getting too invested in the idea you might actually get your life straightened out."

"I have fame, fortune, success… What more do you want from me?"

Ethan looked at Brady, who merely shrugged. "At the risk of sounding maudlin, which I will blame on too much alcohol, we just want you to be happy."

"I *am*, damn it." He slammed his hand on the table, causing poker chips to jump.

"We can tell."

"Bite me." Finn went to the fridge behind the bar for another beer.

Brady turned in his chair to face him. "So if you're so happy what's all this about?"

Finn sorted through several answers, and when none of them seemed right, shrugged instead.

"Did you see that?" Brady nudged Ethan. "Aspyn was right."

Ethan nodded. "I thought it was just an annoying habit, but I'm going to go with her on this one."

He was going to regret asking, but… "What?"

"Your answer to everything is a shrug," Brady said. "You really don't seem to care. No wonder Caitlyn keeps leaving you. No matter what happens, you shrug it off."

"Because there's very little in life that's truly life or death. Everything else will sort itself out in time."

"And it makes you look like you really don't give a damn."

What had Cait said? *People believe what they see.* Now his brothers were piling on, too. "I care when it's worth caring about."

Ethan nudged Brady. "I like Caitlyn—"

"You don't even know Cait," Finn interrupted.

"I know she's got guts. Most people wouldn't have the courage to try to redeem themselves and make a comeback. They'd just slink away into obscurity."

Brady nodded. "True. That does show guts."

"And she probably would have done fine if I'd left her alone."

"Then why didn't you?" Brady asked.

Finn started to shrug, but caught himself. "Because I wanted her." He came back to the table and sat.

Ethan leaned forward and propped his elbows on the table. "I think she's proved she wants you, too."

"She says I'm a drug."

Brady's eyebrows pulled together. "That's new."

Ethan was nodding, though, as if he agreed with Cait. "I'd believe that. The allure of drugs is the high. It feels good. And you two certainly seem to have a hard time staying away from each other."

"Then I just don't understand her. Life is short. Do what feels good."

"Sure," Brady added. "But how many people do you know that went into rehab?"

"A few. But Cait isn't an addict."

Ethan rubbed his eyes. "I've had too much to drink to play with metaphors, so let me explain this to you in small words. If she says you're a drug, it means that as much as she wants you, she doesn't think you're good for her."

Finn fiddled with his poker chips. "She's made that much very clear. And look—it seems she's right. Her life seems to spin into hell every time she gets near me."

"Then you have to show her that you are good for her. That you can be good for each other."

"And how exactly do I do that?"

"By offering her what she needs."

"I don't know what the hell she needs. I don't think she

does, either. One minute she's planning her great redemption story—which doesn't star me—and the next she's deciding she'd rather play the tragic heroine. Also without me, I might add." He rubbed a hand over his face. Once again, Cait was the great paradox of his existence. There were scores of people lined up to tell him what he could do for them, what they needed from him. But not Cait. She didn't want or need anything he had to offer. "Lord, if anyone is a drug it's her. She's messed with my brain enough."

Ethan rolled his eyes. "Then suck it up and quit acting like an idiot."

"Gee, thanks."

Brady flipped a poker chip at him. "Ethan's right. And he knows from experience. So do I, actually. You're certainly carrying on a family tradition."

Ethan laughed. "It must be in the DNA. You know, we *do* suck at psychology. We were doing an intervention for the wrong thing."

"I don't have a clue what the two of you are talking about."

"The great Marshall failing is arrogance," Brady explained. "Taken to the extreme, you'll end up like our father. It makes for good politicians, but lousy people. We were trying to save you from that."

"We were totally barking up the wrong tree." Ethan shook his head sadly.

"Well, I'm glad you admit it." The conversation had taken a wrong turn, and Finn was having a hard time following along. "I still don't see what this has to do with me."

Ethan leaned forward. "Do you want Caitlyn?"

"Yes."

Brady held up a hand. "The more important question is do you love Caitlyn?"

Finn hesitated. How many women had told him he was incapable of that emotion? It certainly wasn't one he was familiar with. He certainly felt *something* for Cait, but was it love?

Ethan saved him from answering. "For the purpose of going forward—and because I really don't want to be at this all night—the judges will accept that as a yes."

"And...?"

Brady went to the bar and got two more beers. He returned to the table and handed one to Ethan. "Then pay attention, little brother, 'cause your big brothers are about to teach you something very important."

"And what would that be?"

Ethan grinned. "How to grovel."

CHAPTER ELEVEN

FINN had never been so happy to hand something over to the post-production team. And he didn't realize how much *Folly* had been weighing on him until he did so. He wanted to be in the editing room, but he was honest enough to admit that editing was not his forte, and he'd be more in the way than anything else. Both Farrell and the editor, Paul, shared his vision for *Folly* and he had confidence in their work.

But he'd check in in a couple of weeks, regardless. Just to be sure.

He sat on his balcony, watching the waves lap the Malibu shore. Once back in the controlled setting of a studio, the last weeks of filming had gone quickly and without catastrophe. Without Cait around, his stress level had decreased substantially, mainly because Naomi had chilled out as well. As expected, the hoopla had died down as soon as Cait left for New York. Almost immediately, there'd been something else to take its place, and while Finn knew it wasn't forgotten, it was no longer hot news.

The last few weeks had been successful and easy, yet oddly boring.

Three scripts for potential new projects, a preliminary plan for a New York expansion of Dolfinn, and a budget for the next project lay on the table next to his chair. He was studiously and deliberately ignoring them all.

Because, according to the buzz, Cait was finally back in town. Which meant it was time for him to make a decision. He had to put up or shut up. And, since he was utterly miserable, it was looking more likely like he'd have to put up. Possibly even tonight, because tonight was *Folly*'s wrap party.

He had no idea if Cait was planning to show or not.

Contrary to her statement before she left Baltimore, Cait was remaining rather low-key at the moment: shopping on Rodeo Drive, lunching in all the proper spots and slipping back into her birthright as if she'd never left. She wasn't flying under the radar, but she wasn't calling undue attention to herself, either. She was just letting it be known that she was back. While she was currently staying at her parents' house in Beverly Hills, she'd been spotted house-hunting not far from here, making the statement she was back to stay without saying a single word.

Especially to him. *He* had to get his news on Cait from the media, the same as everyone else. It was frustrating.

Her agent was also letting it be known that Cait was actively seeking a new project, but when a casting director for Dolfinn's next picture had sent over a script perfect for Cait, he'd been turned down.

Finn wasn't sure if that was personal or not.

And it bothered him that it might be. She was certainly avoiding him. He'd remained cautiously optimistic that Cait would get in touch once she'd had some quality time to think and cool down. That hadn't happened. Now she'd arrived back in L.A., he figured they were bound to run into each other eventually, and he could let things happen naturally, but *eventually* was taking way too long and his patience was at its end. He was going to have to make the move, and for the first time in his life he wasn't sure how he was going to handle it.

His evening with Brady and Ethan had resulted in a painful hangover the next morning, but it was the hard truths that bothered him the most.

Brady had asked him if he loved Cait. He'd hesitated at the time, but now he was sure. He missed her. There'd been a hole in his life the last three years, only he hadn't known it. Or hadn't admitted it. Now he not only admitted it, he knew the cause. He needed her to feel complete.

And when he'd nearly thrown a punch last week at that stupid reporter who'd hounded him about Cait he'd known for sure. He didn't care what they said about him, but he cared what they said about her. And not only because she cared so much. It was the first time he'd worried about what the press was going to say about him. About them.

It was a giant mess. He and Cait were destined to live out their lives in the tabloids. They'd made that choice when they chose their careers. And since they'd be in the press separately or together, he'd rather it be together. The trick would be convincing Cait that it wouldn't be the worst thing ever.

So much for those people who thought he didn't give a damn about anything or anyone.

He gave a damn about Cait. And it was killing him.

One way or the other, *something* had to give. And if Cait didn't show tonight—well, tomorrow he'd turn stalker and go find her. The stalemate had gone on long enough.

Caitlyn took a deep breath as she smoothed out the shimmery fabric of her dress. Julio had done them both proud with this creation. It draped perfectly off her shoulders, showing plenty of collarbone and just a hint of cleavage. Nipping in at her waist and somehow managing to make it look several inches smaller, the dress stopped just short enough to draw plenty of attention. With a pair of simple black stilettos and her hair twisted into loose curls, she hit the sweet spot between dressy and casual, landing perfectly between look-at-me! and low-key.

Julio was a genius, and, even more importantly, had welcomed her back with open arms, calling her his muse. The truth was that Julio had many muses, but he knew that anything he put on Caitlyn would get plenty of attention. He made her look her best, and she guaranteed him more free advertising than anyone else. It was a win-win situation.

Caitlyn certainly needed the boost of a fabulous dress if she was actually going to attend the wrap party for *Folly*. Everything had been going so well since her return to town that she really hated to revisit the disaster. But she was damned either way. If she went, everyone would speculate there was more to the story, and they'd replay everything from Baltimore to remind the public how juicy it all was. If she didn't go, they'd *still* replay everything from Baltimore, only this time it would play out as being so scandalous she didn't dare show her face at the wrap party.

She really wished there was a very good, very public reason she needed to be elsewhere tonight. Honestly, it seemed rather anticlimactic to attend a wrap party now, weeks after her involvement with the film had ended. But it would be rude to the rest of the cast and crew not to go. Plus, it was well-known that Dolfinn threw some of the best parties in the industry. If she wanted to be seen as a major player, she needed to be at the parties with the major players.

Even if one of them was Finn.

She'd spent a lot of time recently very studiously not thinking about Finn. It wasn't helping all that much; her chest still hurt and her arms still ached. Like everything else, that would pass in time. *I have to keep telling myself that. Pretty soon I'll believe it.*

She wasn't asking for the moon. She just wanted to come first with someone for once, before the film and the press and everything else that shouted for attention all the time. Years of therapy had given her acceptance as far as her parents were concerned, but she wanted more than that from Finn. She couldn't live with anything less.

Dolfinn had rented out one of the clubs on Sunset, and the band of paparazzi and fans staking out the doors turned *en masse* as her limo pulled to the curb. She checked her hair and put a smile on her face as the driver opened the door.

Several photographers shouted her name, and she turned to pose and wave at the cameras. She even signed an autograph or two. Yep, this was her life. She was home.

Why did it leave her feeling rather flat?

Walter Farrell caught her in a hug as she walked inside. "Good to see you, Caitlyn." He tucked her arm in his. "It was absolutely wonderful working with you. I've got a script I want you to read."

"Have your assistant send it over. I'd love to look at it." *Score one point.* The director not only wanted to work with her again, he already had a project in mind. Enough people had overhead Walter's words to ensure that info would make the rounds quick enough. Maybe her comeback wasn't going to be as rocky as she'd imagined.

Then someone was pressing a champagne flute into her hand, and the atmosphere became party-like. This was the part of wrap parties she really liked: the chance to actually meet the people who made it all work while they weren't all busy *making* it work.

When a rep from the distribution company pulled her aside to talk about a couple of opportunities beyond her normal press junket schedule, her personal disaster seemed to be paying off professionally. It hadn't been fun, but maybe it had been worth it.

Even Dolby seemed happy to see her. "I've sneaked a peek,

and it's fantastic. Make sure that new house has a mantel for all the trophies."

"I'll do that."

"And I'm glad you came tonight. Some people seemed to think you wouldn't."

She'd bet Naomi—who was on the other side of the room, pretending she didn't know Caitlyn was even there—was one of those people. Oh, she was glad she'd come, after all, if for no other reason than to tick off Naomi. It was juvenile, but she'd get her thrills where she could.

"I wouldn't have missed it for anything."

Though she kept the smile on her face, Dolby's comment had dampened the pleasure of the evening for her a bit. While the hoopla in the press had died down, it *did* bother her that her peers and colleagues might still be gossiping about her behind her back. She could handle the changing opinions of the public, but professionally she didn't want the taint and the awkwardness.

The crowd was dense, the sheer number of people responsible for this project showing the scope and difficulty of getting this story to the screen. Thankfully, the crowd kept her busy and away from Finn. She couldn't fully enjoy herself because the tension of knowing he was there and that she'd have to run into him eventually put a knot in her stomach.

"Eventually" came a little quicker than she'd have liked. She was chatting with the armorer, who she'd worked with years ago on another film. Since the battle scenes had been filmed on the studio's back lot in L.A., this was the first she'd seen him since. Mid-sentence, she saw Finn out of the corner of her eye.

In black pants and a casual gray shirt, he looked like the star of the film instead of its producer. His hair had the perfect casual tousle that other men had to work to achieve, and the overhead lights caught the blond highlights. His tan was deeper; obviously he'd been back on the beach since his return. She couldn't quite see who he was talking to, but he laughed at something and the smile nearly weakened her knees.

All in all, he looked good enough to eat with a spoon in slow bites, and something inside her ached. It was beyond unfair to want something she couldn't have so badly. And it *hurt*. She had the sudden urge to go back to London. It was much easier to get over someone when they were five thousand miles away—it was like ripping off the bandage quickly. The fact he looked so completely unaffected just rubbed salt in the wound.

Being back here in the same town was just going to drag out the pain and make it even more difficult.

She knew the second Finn spotted her. She could almost feel his eyes on her. But she would be safe for a few more minutes. She'd have time to prepare herself. It wasn't as if Finn could just stop what he was doing and come over here—

"Cait."

But I could be wrong.

Very aware that everyone was watching and trying to listen, even as they pretended they weren't, she forced herself to smile. She even managed to lift her cheek for the mandatory air kiss next to her cheek. "Finn. It's good to see you. Dolfinn throws great parties."

He started to say something, but stopped, his eyes cutting to the crowd that was only just managing to pretend to be uninterested. She could almost see Finn change his mind about what he was going to say. *That was a first.*

His jaw was tight, but his words were casual enough. "Are you enjoying being home?"

"Yes, I am, thanks. I'm still figuring out where the best new restaurants are, but it's good to be back."

"Try Intaglios on Santa Monica. You'll like the fish."

She nodded, but the sheer inanity of the conversation had her biting her lip so as not to laugh. Finn noticed, and his jaw loosened a little as well.

"And how are your parents?"

It was a loaded question, but one she was prepared for. "They're happy to have me home, of course, and looking forward to the premiere. They're quite proud, actually."

Finn nodded in understanding. "Glad to hear it."

Their audience had noted their boring small talk and moved back to their own conversations once she and Finn didn't deliver fireworks immediately. The noise level began to return to its earlier level.

Finn dropped his voice a notch. "You look good, Cait. One of Julio's creations?"

"Of course. *He's* certainly glad I'm back."

"You're keeping a low profile these days."

She sipped at her champagne casually. "I'm trying to get settled. You know, get my bearings again."

"Planning your big splash?"

Oh, she knew exactly what he was referring to. "I'm keeping all my options open at the moment."

"That seems like a wise decision."

"I have been known to make those occasionally. I try to learn from my mistakes." She hadn't meant that as a jab, but Finn seemed to receive it as such. She wasn't going to take it back or try to explain, though. Retreat, however, seemed to be a viable and smart option. "I think I'll go refill my drink."

"I'll go with you."

"I don't think that's wise."

"I don't care."

"Why am I not surprised?" she snapped, and Finn had the gall to look offended. She quickly adjusted her smile and attitude so as not to attract attention. "Look, this really isn't the time or place. There are too many people, too many cameras. I don't want to—"

"Come on." Finn stepped to his left, out of the main room into a side hallway. When she didn't follow, Finn's mouth tightened and he returned to bend close to her ear. "You know I don't care one way or the other who witnesses what, but I know *you* do. I want to talk to you—alone—and I have no problem carrying you out of here if I have to. Your choice."

It certainly wasn't much of a choice. She was well aware Finn would do it, too, if she pushed him. *Might as well get this over with.* She'd let him say whatever was so God-awful important and then go about her merry way.

She sat her drink on a table and squared her shoulders. "Fine," she conceded, following him into the hall. "Let's just get this over with."

Finn pushed open a door directly to her right and nearly hauled her inside. She was sputtering with outrage as he flipped on a light and she realized they were in a storeroom of some sort. He closed the door behind him and stood in front of it, blocking any chance of escape.

Getting her feet under her, she adjusted her dress back into place. "I swear, Finn, you are *this* close to getting slapped again."

"If it will make you feel better, do it." He lifted his chin in a dare.

Caitlyn suddenly realized how small and quiet this room was. Facing Finn while surrounded by a hundred people had seemed an impossible feat, yet she'd managed. But here…? There was barely two feet between them because Finn's big body took up most of the space. She could smell him, feel the body heat radiating off him… She took a step back and found herself against a shelf.

Trying to act casual, even if she didn't quite feel it, she leaned against it and crossed her arms over her chest.

Indicating the liquor bottles around them, she shook her head. "I'd end up breaking something if I took a swing at you, and I don't want to add property damage to this fiasco. But it would serve you right if I did."

His voice and face softened. "Are you ready to talk to me now?"

Stay strong. "There's nothing to talk about, Finn."

"I disagree."

"Of course you do." She'd meant it to sound snappy and sarcastic, but it came out tired instead. *Damn.* "There seems to be very little we agree on anymore."

Finn's response was to kiss her. There was no warning, no time to think, just a flash of movement and then Finn's mouth was on hers, his body pressing close. It was like throwing a match on a stack of kindling: a moment of stillness followed by a *whoomph* as it caught and burned.

This was what haunted her dreams. The feel of Finn's lips, the way the energy moved from him through her and back again. She could taste desire and want, but beyond that there was a feeling of calm and *rightness*. Which was wrong.

Caitlyn broke the kiss and fought for control. "The last time someone tried that I brought him to his knees."

"You frequently bring me to my knees."

Finn rested his forehead against hers as she tried to process his words. His hands moved from her arms to grip the shelf on either side of her shoulders. She could easily duck under and escape, but for reasons that she didn't want to explore too deeply at the moment, she stayed where she was.

"And it was a risk I was willing to take," he added.

"Why?"

"Because I wanted to remind you why you should listen to me." He lifted his head from hers and grinned as he tucked a lock of hair behind her ear. "And because I like kissing you. I've missed that."

"You are an arrogant, conceited—"

"And you are stubborn, frustrating and..." he paused as he traced a finger over her jaw, causing her breath to hitch slightly "...perfect."

She'd done dozens of scenes where the hero said or did something that melted the heroine's heart—and she'd pulled them off—but now she knew what it was *supposed* to feel like: a warm squeeze that tapered off into a shiver, leaving her heart in her throat and her eyes burning.

She wanted to say something snarky and snappy, putting him in his place. The words wouldn't come. "I don't think I can do this, Finn." Her hand was cupping his jaw. Once she realized it, she let her hand drop and looked away. "We've struck out twice already."

"Then we still have one more try."

"I can't go through it again. It's too much. Too hard." Her voice cracked a little. "And it hurts too bad to walk away from you."

"Then maybe you should quit walking away."

She looked up and stared him down. "You've never given me a good reason to stay."

"I love you."

Caitlyn felt slightly faint.

Finn watched the color drain from Cait's face as her eyes widened. She even swayed a bit before she steadied herself. Maybe he'd gone a step too far. Maybe he'd misread the entire situation and gone all in on an empty hand.

Either way, Cait wasn't exactly showing joy at his spontaneous declaration.

But she'd kissed him back, and was currently standing in his arms instead of bolting for the door, so that had to mean something.

At least he hoped so.

"Cait?"

She blinked and blew out her breath. "That's…new."

Between what he'd expected to hear and what he'd hoped to hear… Well, that was neither. He couldn't say he hadn't been warned, though. Brady and Ethan were being proved right, damn it.

"It's not a new feeling, Cait. I just figured out the words."

"You can't be in love with me."

Another answer he hadn't expected. "Why not?"

"You don't let people get close to you. Not like that."

He toyed with a lock of hair that fell over her shoulder. "You're right. You're definitely the first."

She sighed and her shoulders dropped in defeat. "I can't."

"Because…?"

"Love is… Love is… It's supposed to be comfortable, easy."

"I can't decide if you've watched too many movies or not enough of them."

Her lips pressed into a thin line. "I'm serious. We have a good time together, but I'm not sure we're really good for each other. It's like we're—"

He tightened his fingers on the shelf to keep his temper under control. "If you bring up drugs and addiction one more time—"

"But it's true."

"No, it's not. An addiction shows a weakness for something you shouldn't have or don't need. Finding someone to lean on isn't an addiction."

"Well, it's not exactly healthy, either."

"That's ridiculous. I love you for you. It's simple. I *want* you to lean on me."

"But before—"

"You think I don't know that you thought being yourself wasn't good enough for your parents and that ridiculous idea of a birthright? I have a legacy, too, but DNA is not destiny. We've both proved that. The more you beat yourself up over it, the more you needed to escape the disappointment. It became a self-fulfilling prophecy. But I wasn't the cause. I was just the outlet." He paused to rub a hand over her hair. "And I'm okay with that. Whatever you need, I want to be that for you."

Cait's eyes widened with each word, and when they couldn't go any farther her mouth dropped open as well. He'd laugh, except his own response was rather similar. He'd surprised himself with that little impassioned speech.

Closing her mouth with a snap, Cait cleared her throat. "That's a really sweet, wonderful and…" her mouth quirked "…kinda cheesy thing to say."

"I obviously spend too much time with bad scripts. But the sentiment is real." He cleared his throat. "And one you haven't reciprocated. Yet."

"I've always loved you, Finn." She said it quietly, without meeting his eyes, and he didn't realize he'd been holding his breath until she finally said the words. "Which is why it's been so hard to be back. To be around you. I thought you didn't care."

"There are a lot of things I *don't* care about. But I do care about you. If you want me to sue the tabloids for slander and invasion of privacy, I will. There are plenty of attorneys in my family with nothing better to do than keep the media tied up in lawsuits for decades. I'll have my father call Congressional hearings if it will make you happy. If you want me to buy billboards or skywrite, I can do that, too. Whatever it takes to prove it to you. Honestly, I don't give a rat's ass what anyone thinks of me or mine, because it's a waste of energy I could use on something far more fun or important, but whatever is important to you is important to me. And if that means I have to take on the media or whoever, I will. Hell, I'll buy all the damn magazines out if you want."

"You'd do that for me?"

"More, actually. Just tell me what you want."

"But why?"

"Because I need you. We may not be good for each other in the normal sense, but we're not normal people. We don't live in a normal world. You are the one thing that really matters to me. Nothing else. And I'll be happy to prove that however you want."

Cait swallowed hard. "Wow."

"You keep saying that."

"Because this is a whole new Finn."

"Same Finn. I'm just making a few things clear to you this time around."

Her smile was blinding. "I appreciate your efforts. That's all I really needed to hear."

"And?"

Cait ducked under his arm and reached for the door. That was not what he'd expected, and he grabbed for her elbow. "Cait, wait—"

As she opened the door the sound of the party intruded. "I can't carry you, but I will drag you if necessary. It would be easier if you'd just follow me."

She extended her hand and he took it. At that moment, his world finally righted and made sense. "Anywhere."

Every head turned in their direction as they exited the closet, but Cait merely grinned at the crowds parting in shock in front of her as she walked toward the front doors of the restaurant with him dogging her heels.

The paparazzi were still four deep behind the roped-off entranceway, and his and Cait's sudden appearance brought a barrage of shouted questions and blinding flashes.

Without a word, Cait threw herself into his arms and planted her lips on his.

And he totally forgot the cameras were there.

Not that he cared, anyway.

EPILOGUE

"HERE we go." Caitlyn grabbed the remote and turned up the volume, nudging Finn until he put down the script he was reading.

"I thought you hated Carrie Catner."

She dropped down beside him on the couch, settling in to the corner, and draped her legs across Finn's lap. "I do. With the heat of a thousand suns. I just want to know if she's going to hatchet me to death again tonight."

"She wouldn't dare."

She appreciated the show of loyalty, but Carrie Catner seemed to live to criticize her these days. Oddly, though, it didn't bother her all that much. She still wanted to know what was said, though.

"Self-appointed fashion police annoy me."

"You looked amazing last night, and even she couldn't say otherwise." He leaned over to give her a kiss.

The intro to *The Catner Report* played and Carrie's overly perky face filled the screen. "Last night's Los Angeles pre-miere of the much-awaited World War II drama *The Folly of the Fury* was a star-studded event. Fans of both the book and the stars were lined up around the block. Even some of Washington's VIPs were on hand to honor former US Senator Porter Marshall, to whom the film was dedicated, and who was instrumental in getting the much-loved book to the screen."

"Aw, your Grands look adorable."

Finn nodded, a small smile playing around his mouth. His hand smoothed along the outside of her thigh.

"The film's stars, Jason Elkins and Naomi Harte, seemed on friendly enough terms, calling into question recent reports that the two had a falling out shortly after filming."

Caitlyn was livid. "Nothing about *her* dress? Naomi's stylist must have been high to put her in that sack. Even I felt bad for her."

"Of course star-watchers know that the true trouble on set was between Harte and supporting actress Caitlyn Reese over the film's producer, Finn Marshall."

Caitlyn stuck out her tongue at the screen. "Yeah, yeah, we all know. Old news."

Finally the clips of her and Finn began to roll, and Carrie's voice picked up urgency. "Reese and Marshall arrived at the premiere in the company of her parents, director John Reese and actress Margaret Fields-Reese, and Senator and Mrs. Marshall. The continuing romance between the children of both Hollywood's and Washington's most powerful and influential families have positioned the pair as a rising power all their own. While the couple makes regular appearances around town and are sharing a Malibu beach house, they've kept quiet on any future plans. However, Marshall was recently spotted at Harry Winston on Rodeo Drive—"

Finn cursed and grabbed for the remote. Caitlyn smacked his hands away and turned the volume up another notch.

"—and an anonymous source claims he was examining engagement rings. While a purchase *was* made—and we can't say for certain it was a ring—careful examination of Reese's hands last night showed no sign of anything large and sparkly."

Finn grabbed for the remote again, and this time she let him have it. Not that she could have stopped him in her semi-shocked state. He silenced the TV as her heart seemed to stutter in her chest. She kept her cool, though, and merely looked at him expectantly. He looked distinctly uncomfortable.

She finally had to break the silence. "You were shopping at Harry Winston? After a new watch or something?"

Finn sighed. Lifting her legs with one hand, he arched his hips and reached into his jeans pocket. "It was supposed to be a surprise, you know. With some flowers and wine or something."

She swallowed hard as Finn resettled and balanced a box on her knee. "I'm still quite surprised."

Finn cracked the box and the sides opened like wings.

Whoa. Holy... Caitlyn knew her eyes had to be popping out of her head, but she kept her hands in her lap. "Wow. That's certainly *not* a watch."

Finn's eyebrows pulled together. "Cait..."

"But it's beautiful."

He removed the ring and held it with his fingertips. From the look on his face, Finn seemed to be having a hard time choosing his words. Finally he sighed. "Do I have to ask?"

"It would be nice." She bit back a laugh at his discomfort. "Just so that we're clear, you know?"

That earned her a frown. "*Clearly*, I'm hoping that you'll marry me."

She frowned back at him. "I can't say yes unless you ask."

"You don't get the ring until you do," he teased.

"Then we're going to be here a while."

Finn grinned. "Do you have something better to do?"

She shifted a little closer and ran her hand over his chest.

She felt the muscles jump and his heartbeat kick up as she pressed a kiss to his neck. "Maybe."

"That's cheating."

She shrugged. "I don't really care."

* * * * *

Mills & Boon® Hardback

April 2012

ROMANCE

A Deal at the Altar	Lynne Graham
Return of the Moralis Wife	Jacqueline Baird
Gianni's Pride	Kim Lawrence
Undone by his Touch	Annie West
The Legend of de Marco	Abby Green
Stepping out of the Shadows	Robyn Donald
Deserving of his Diamonds?	Melanie Milburne
Girl Behind the Scandalous Reputation	Michelle Conder
Redemption of a Hollywood Starlet	Kimberly Lang
Cracking the Dating Code	Kelly Hunter
The Cattle King's Bride	Margaret Way
Inherited: Expectant Cinderella	Myrna Mackenzie
The Man Who Saw Her Beauty	Michelle Douglas
The Last Real Cowboy	Donna Alward
New York's Finest Rebel	Trish Wylie
The Fiancée Fiasco	Jackie Braun
Sydney Harbour Hospital: Tom's Redemption	Fiona Lowe
Summer With A French Surgeon	Margaret Barker

HISTORICAL

Dangerous Lord, Innocent Governess	Christine Merrill
Captured for the Captain's Pleasure	Ann Lethbridge
Brushed by Scandal	Gail Whitiker
Lord Libertine	Gail Ranstrom

MEDICAL

Georgie's Big Greek Wedding?	Emily Forbes
The Nurse's Not-So-Secret Scandal	Wendy S. Marcus
Dr Right All Along	Joanna Neil
Doctor on Her Doorstep	Annie Claydon

ROMANCE

Jewel in His Crown	Lynne Graham
The Man Every Woman Wants	Miranda Lee
Once a Ferrara Wife...	Sarah Morgan
Not Fit for a King?	Jane Porter
Snowbound with Her Hero	Rebecca Winters
Flirting with Italian	Liz Fielding
Firefighter Under the Mistletoe	Melissa McClone
The Tycoon Who Healed Her Heart	Melissa James

HISTORICAL

The Lady Forfeits	Carole Mortimer
Valiant Soldier, Beautiful Enemy	Diane Gaston
Winning the War Hero's Heart	Mary Nichols
Hostage Bride	Anne Herries

MEDICAL

Breaking Her No-Dates Rule	Emily Forbes
Waking Up With Dr Off-Limits	Amy Andrews
Tempted by Dr Daisy	Caroline Anderson
The Fiancée He Can't Forget	Caroline Anderson
A Cotswold Christmas Bride	Joanna Neil
All She Wants For Christmas	Annie Claydon

Mills & Boon® Hardback

May 2012

ROMANCE

A Vow of Obligation	Lynne Graham
Defying Drakon	Carole Mortimer
Playing the Greek's Game	Sharon Kendrick
One Night in Paradise	Maisey Yates
His Majesty's Mistake	Jane Porter
Duty and the Beast	Trish Morey
The Darkest of Secrets	Kate Hewitt
Behind the Castello Doors	Chantelle Shaw
The Morning After The Wedding Before	Anne Oliver
Never Stay Past Midnight	Mira Lyn Kelly
Valtieri's Bride	Caroline Anderson
Taming the Lost Prince	Raye Morgan
The Nanny Who Kissed Her Boss	Barbara McMahon
Falling for Mr Mysterious	Barbara Hannay
One Day to Find a Husband	Shirley Jump
The Last Woman He'd Ever Date	Liz Fielding
Sydney Harbour Hospital: Lexi's Secret	Melanie Milburne
West Wing to Maternity Wing!	Scarlet Wilson

HISTORICAL

Lady Priscilla's Shameful Secret	Christine Merrill
Rake with a Frozen Heart	Marguerite Kaye
Miss Cameron's Fall from Grace	Helen Dickson
Society's Most Scandalous Rake	Isabelle Goddard

MEDICAL

Diamond Ring for the Ice Queen	Lucy Clark
No.1 Dad in Texas	Dianne Drake
The Dangers of Dating Your Boss	Sue MacKay
The Doctor, His Daughter and Me	Leonie Knight

Mills & Boon® Large Print

May 2012

ROMANCE

The Man Who Risked It All — Michelle Reid
The Sheikh's Undoing — Sharon Kendrick
The End of her Innocence — Sara Craven
The Talk of Hollywood — Carole Mortimer
Master of the Outback — Margaret Way
Their Miracle Twins — Nikki Logan
Runaway Bride — Barbara Hannay
We'll Always Have Paris — Jessica Hart

HISTORICAL

The Lady Confesses — Carole Mortimer
The Dangerous Lord Darrington — Sarah Mallory
The Unconventional Maiden — June Francis
Her Battle-Scarred Knight — Meriel Fuller

MEDICAL

The Child Who Rescued Christmas — Jessica Matthews
Firefighter With A Frozen Heart — Dianne Drake
Mistletoe, Midwife...Miracle Baby — Anne Fraser
How to Save a Marriage in a Million — Leonie Knight
Swallowbrook's Winter Bride — Abigail Gordon
Dynamite Doc or Christmas Dad? — Marion Lennox